T0209107

S.S. SIMPSON

CAMOUFLAGE

authorHOUSE®

AuthorHouse™
1663 Liberty Drive
Bloomington, IN 47403
www.authorhouse.com
Phone: 1 (800) 839-8640

Published by AuthorHouse 12/03/2019

ISBN: 978-1-7283-3848-4 (sc)
ISBN: 978-1-7283-3847-7 (e)

CONTENTS

DEDICATION

To the broken and desperate whom only God can

THE SMOKING GLOVE

Baseball: the air that I breathed, the dirt that I stood in, the mitt that I clutched. Out here, everything mattered. I knew who I was. Today was the big day, the playoffs that determined who would play in the state finals.

The disgusted batter from the opposite team turned around and prepared me, "You wait, you just wait. See what mincemeat I make out of you."

All the while I knew what he said was true. I was a behind the scenes man, a terrific catcher but put me up at bat, and I crumbled like brown sugar on a coffee cake.

Changing sides, our team members slapped one another affectionately. Sure enough the kid that Samuel just struck out was their pitcher. He had more moves than Samuel. I was certain that I wouldn't have to face him. I was very wrong. Bases were loaded. Everyone held their breath wondering who was going to have to shoulder the victory home.

Mr. Robson, our coach, looked around, bit his lip and called out my name He must have been in a self-induced trance and just called out the wrong name. Gazing at me quizzically, he patted me here and there making sure that I was in one piece.

Like radar the pitcher's eyes sliced through me. The ball whizzed toward me. Gasping. I stared the spinning ball down, then remembered that I had to hit it.

Mr. Robson, yelled, "Keep your eye on the ball, it's yours CJ." Where else would my eyes be? Chanting, screaming, jumping, and shaking the stands, the kids from school filled the bleachers to the brim. But I couldn't help but notice that my biggest fan, my dad, wasn't there. Where was he?

1

This was his life. He always told me that I was a chip off the old baseball block and would become the infamous baseball signer that he so wanted to be.

It was a clean hit over the top. As I dropped the cracked bat all I heard was the chanted word,' run' and I did. Bases were overloaded. Adrenalin rushed into my mouth, ears, eyes, arms, and legs. My legs became supernatural. The whitish bases faded with mixed orange clay. All I saw were the agonized faces of the base's guardians who were determined that I would not pass. I didn't; I flew by. One after the other the bases faded behind me. Home plate was wiped clean waiting my footsteps. Before I felt it, I heard it. It was an eerie sound; unlike anything that I had heard before. One minute I was a running gazelle, the next minute everything slowed and stopped. It hit and I collapsed into empty darkness.

"Where was Mr. Sanger? Where was the kid's dad? Give him air, call an ambulance. Who knew CPR? "He wasn't breathing. Mr. Robson also gulped for air. CJ was his adopted son, a boy with his spirit, a young man who never gave up. He wasn't going to lose him.

When CJ first tried out for the team, he couldn't swing a bat or throw a pitch. Every day CJ showed up, hauled buckets of water back and forth and watched the team practice from the dug-out. Much to Mr. Robson's amazement, CJ went from water boy to a member of the team after practicing endless hours of hitting, catching, and pitching with his patient dad. Mr. Robson was an over-due eruption. His pent-up anger exploded.

"Hey, Sims, is that the way you teach your boys to throw a ball, to take the player down, to take the very breath out of him? Would you like to know how it feels?"

Coach Sims spat right in front of Mr. Robson's sneakers. "Put your fist where your mouth is."

To the horror of all, the two coaches became seventh graders. Tight fists flew in every direction. Rushing out, the boys supported their frazzled coaches and added their own fists to the ruckus. Fuming parents grabbed their kids. Pandemonium had its way. The cops were called.

Wobbling back toward CJ, Mr. Robson heard BJ, the baseball –want-a- be, administer CPR. Every day BJ asked him why she couldn't play on the team. Every day he made up an excuse. All excuses vanished; BJ would wear the team's shirt just like the rest of them.

"Until help comes, I will stay with CJ." BJ knew CPR and coached herself along. As if on assignment, BJ pushed, counted, and breathed, waiting for CJ's chest to rise and fall on its own. It did. Wide, grateful eyes watched and commended her. Mr. Robson's eyes confirmed that she was now part of the team.

As I opened my eyes, everything swirled around me. It must be heaven because the lips of most beautiful girl I ever saw were sealed with mine. Her brownish tinted eyes matched her wavy, brownish, playful hair. She was the one who was always in the bleachers during baseball practice.

"Are we in heaven?" BJ smirked.

"No, we are right here on earth where we belong for the time being."

"I know you; you are that girl, our undeclared mascot, the one who cheers us on."

"Yes, yes I am. But you need to stop talking and just concentrate on breathing. You blacked out for a while and you need to rest."

Closing my eyes, I sank back into heaven, wanting to see my dad. Where ever we were, I was certain that my dad could talk his way into getting a pass. After all he was the top salesman at his company.

The ambulance's siren pierced through the afternoon air. The attendants were confused why the two coaches were handcuffed and led away. Red-faced and embarrassed, the obsessed parents escorted their kids off the school yard and made up excuses for what just happened.

The attendants spied CJ. Reluctantly, BJ gave up her post

"You have done a great job. His vital signs are good and he is breathing steadily. I don't think that we even need to take him with us."

"Oh, what good news," answered Mrs. Post whose son, Terin, also carried a mitt and was a member of CJ's scattered baseball team. Barging in, Mrs. Post knelt down next to CJ.

"Can he speak?" Without waiting for an answer, Mrs. Post's quickened words rambled. "CJ, don't worry son; I'm here and everything will be okay. Your dad was called away and wanted you to know that I will stay with you."

"But where's my dad? He has never missed a single game."

Terin jumped in. "CJ It's like this. There was just no way that your dad could make it. He's in the hospital."

Mrs. Post paled at the directness of her son.

CJ winced. "The hospital?" Get up I told myself. I could breathe. Could my dad? That was the only thing that I wanted to know.

Before I could ask what happened, we all piled carefully into Mrs. Post's shiny just waxed, over the top Cadillac Suburban and somehow made it to the hospital. The most beautiful girl in the world didn't even get so much as a thank you. She faded in the background along with baseball as I once knew it.

COLD AND STERILE

T ime halted. Without my dad, I was nothing and might as well be an orphan. My mother didn't even know that I had a game today nor did she care. She probably was out shopping with some of her friends and didn't even know about dad.

Mrs. Post never drove over the speed limit. Today she could have qualified for the Indi 500. Terin and I held on to our seat belts and our fears.

A true blooded teenager, Terin couldn't want to give me the gruesome details. "Somebody ran your dad off the road; a kid, an older kid. Your dad drove the car into a ditch and the very breath was kicked out of the car. Just like what happened to you. They managed to pull your dad out of the wreckage but no one knows how he is."

At that instant, I hated Terin, his tone of voice, his innuendos, and his flippant nature. Curling my fist in his face, I almost socked him. In the hospital, maybe there was an available bed next to my dad. Maybe I would put Terin in it.

Mrs. Post intervened. "CJ, I just know that your father is all right. On the phone, your mother sounded like she always did. She just didn't want you to worry. Your father is in the best of hands." Spoken like a true mother, never really saying anything but saying everything.

Dead ahead of us was the waiting room. The three of us marched ahead listening to our own drummer. My mother was a scared jack rabbit. She flung her arms around me. Her smudged mascara ran haphazardly down her face.

Exhausted from pretending, Mrs. Post couldn't keep it up any longer. Her pierced heart dropped to the floor. "Robbie, I am really sorry but I need to get Terin home. I can't. I just can't"

"Thank you for bringing me my son. It's enough." Robbie gazed right through Mrs. Post as she clutched her son and scurried out of the room.

The hospital's sterile smell seeped up my nose and made me sick to my stomach. My worst nightmare didn't come close to this. Way down deep inside, I heard my father's voice, "Hold on to mother and don't let her go." I didn't. Every few hours the telephone rang with a brief update just like the weather channel. The only difference was that you couldn't change the channel. The more mother sobbed, the more I didn't. Small and cold, the reception room was a waiting cell. The air hardly moved and the only thing on the wall was a big clock that made sure you knew your loved one's time was running out.

Grabbing mother's hands, we prayed, sang, and prayed childhood prayers that leaped across time. Mother surprised me since we hardly ever prayed at home. The three of us were hardly together in the same house, let alone the same room. My head ached from making so many deals with God. When my dad came out of that operating room, I had many promises to keep. In those six forever hours, I lost all traces of boy hood and became a man. I had to.

Without faked reassurance, Mother never would have made it. The phone rang for the very last time. My dad was off the table. It was finished. The nurse didn't tell us much else, only that he made it, whatever that meant. If I thought the worst was over, I was very wrong.

Dad stayed in the recovery room for the next six hours and there was no weather update. The sofa housed us for the night. Going home was not an option; not even a thought. Tomorrow was Saturday so there was absolutely no reason to move and we didn't.

A young quiet nurse's voice proclaimed, "You may see your husband now. Your dad is right down the hall anxious to see you." Her smile never faded from her face. She must also have a dad that she couldn't live without. "Don't be alarmed. He is very groggy from all of the medication. But he's alive and well, actually a very lucky man. That car did its best to finish him off."

Studying me she stated, "You must be the one that he fought for. If you were my son I wouldn't let you out of my sight." The affectionate nurse led me hand in hand with my mother following down the hall.

"Dad, we're here. We never left." My tears rushed down and saturated my face and Dad's face. His eyes were sealed shut. There was just room enough for me to curl up beside him so I did. His eyes still didn't open but his right arm pulled me to his chest.

"Your mother, where is your mother?"

It had been some time since I saw love, real caring with my parents. Mother looked like she wanted to jump right in next to me. Instead she sat on the bed and held my father's hand. Her tears ran wild, a downpour, worse than mine. Choking, she could hardly speak. Love cried, breathed, and sighed. Dad just grabbed both of our hands and thanked us for loving him.

Exhausted, he completely collapsed and sank back into oblivion. Mother and I hovered for a while until a not so friendly nurse ushered us out of the room. "Enough for today," was all she said. Nurses were like kids, they all looked the same but acted differently.

Gazing at mother's face, I was confused. If she really loved Dad that much why didn't she ever show it? Why didn't she ever say it? Why wasn't she ever home? Why did grownups have such a difficult time telling each other how they felt? Kids sure didn't. One day we were madly in love with one another and the next day we weren't. And we told each other. Maybe it was a different kind of love.

Walking home did me good. Fresh air always had a way of clearing things. My room greeted me. It was still the same. My mitt and my violin were right where I left them. Last night was the very first night that I slept without either one of them. My mitt shared my pillow and my dreams.

A dog was supposed to be a kid's best friend, but I already had one. My violin's strings softly lured me to sleep and I drifted off. Something tugged at me. My dad's face wouldn't leave me. Not once did my dad open up his eyes. The medicine must have shut them. Tomorrow I would see them. But I didn't.

It was early. We were both up. Even though Dad wasn't here, he was everywhere. Suddenly I thought about tomorrow and wondered if there would be one. Very distant, mother wasn't really there. Her eyes darted back and forth as though she expected something. She ate nothing and just looked beyond me. The sadness penetrated her. Both of my parents slipped away from me. I might as well be an orphan.

At the hospital we both took alone time with dad. My parents needed to discuss things that I didn't need to hear. Waiting impatiently, I forced myself to talk to a kid whose dad was also messed up. It helped me knowing that other kids had to deal with exactly what I was going through, the unknown, the fear, the anger. Mother gave me the awaited sign, I was waved in.

Dad was propped up in bed with his leg hoisted up in a sling. He heard my voice and melted. And he reached for my hand where it wasn't.

"CJ, give me your hand. There are some things here that are not what they should be. Yes, I made it son but not all of me made it. It's well, well it's difficult to tell you."

"Dad, dad, you can't see me can you? It's your eyes, your eyes. What did they do to your eyes?" I held my Dad and kissed his eyes.

"My eyes just don't seem to work. Son, they got slammed around in that car and shut tight. My eyes prevented me from seeing and remembering the horror. The nurses told me that it will take time and patience to regain my sight. They mentioned exercises, lots of relearning. Son, to be honest with you, I don't know if I have that patience."

Inside of me, a fearful wild stallion broke loose. Not looking into my Dad's piercing green eyes again was impossible. Not having my Dad watch my baseball games busting with pride was not going to happen. Not seeing my Dad's love was ridiculous. Then and there, I made it my long-term assignment to fix his eyes.

Once I anchored on to something, I held on regardless.

The first step was my intelligent computer. Eye exercises were everywhere. For hours, I printed everything that I could find about eye problems and how to fix them. Eyes were so complicated, so delicate, needed so much care. I never even thought about my eyes. I just expected them to work. The weekend was over and tomorrow was school so I would have to wait to begin my intervention. Mother used to come in and tuck me in now I was the one to tuck her in.

"CJ, I just don't have the energy."

I know, Mom. It's my turn to take care of you. Everything will be okay. You just wait and see." I lied to both of us. Shocking fear was a freight train that vibrated through me. Would it ever come to a stop?

THE MOST BEAUTIFUL
GIRL IN THE WORLD

B ack on the school bus, I was in my neighborhood. Everything was safe; I knew exactly what to expect. The pretty girls with their perfect makeup, streaked hair and designer clothes drooled when I passed their seat. Their eyes begged me to sit down. When I passed the shy girls, they held their breath praying that I wouldn't sit down. Never had a brother, I guess and just being that close to a guy paralyzed them. But once I smiled, the ice bergs usually broke up and drifted down stream.

It was the way her books were tossed all over the seat that intrigued me. She was pretty without the goopy make-up. Her real beauty wasn't masked with a bunch of crazy colors. She seemed younger than the rest. Her eyes looked straight ahead not the least disturbed as I sat down. She was comfortable with her own name since other names like Hillfinger and Polo didn't dance all over her clothes. Her shoes were basic, simple no bows no frills, just sturdy looking. My thoughts surprised me; I didn't sound like a tape recorder of all my friends. There was a brand-new tape in my machine.

"Hey, I'm CJ. I haven't seen you around before. Everything in this town is pretty much just the way it looks. When something is different it stands out. Just look out the window and see for yourself. Most of the houses have at least three chimneys, two fancy cars, and maids running around in dreary outfits taking out the trash, walking dogs, picking up the mail, and entertaining kids. This town couldn't function without them. Our fathers are mostly corporate business men and our mothers are hardly ever home. I guess that's why we know one another so well. We all live the same lives. What do they call you?"

"It's Sarah and thankfully my life is nothing like that. My world centers around the university where my father teaches. We don't need a maid nor do we want one. My sister and I have been brought up to take care of ourselves and that's what we do. My father is my role model. We don't even have a chimney and our one car barely works. I wouldn't change a thing about my life, an adventure that never stops. Because from one day to the next, I never really know where we're going to be and what I'm going to do. Friends are truly ships in the day and night that come and go. I enjoy them when I'm around them. In a moment's notice without my permission, often they are taken from me. We move around a lot."

"For a young kid you sure do a lot of thinking. You should write this down; it would help other kids. Most of us need plenty of help. On the brighter side, being new, you will enjoy our school. The teachers are cool; they have to be. Pretty flexible, they are also easy to flatter, maybe even bribe if you're desperate. Each teacher is hand- picked by a committee, and put through the ringer so to speak. Our parents only want the best teaching us."

"Those PTA meetings can get very loud and intimidating. All the teachers know that they need to watch their back if they want to keep their job. So if you're flunking, most will do anything to pass you. We all know it and get away with most anything."

"Thank you for warning me. You all sound like a bunch of spoiled brats; nothing that I would even want to get to know. It isn't what you are given but what you earn that makes the difference. If the students don't do the work, my dad flunks them regardless. A grade should mean something. And football, baseball, and other sports, is that the reason that most of you go to this school? My father told me that the coaches here are remarkable and state renowned. He wanted me to try out for the tennis team."

"Yup, your dad knew. Without sports, and of course orchestra, I wouldn't be here. Baseball gets me through the day knowing that practice is right after school. When I catch a pitch, my day begins. I don't really work much during classes but on that field, I am a catching machine. In fact, I would do anything the coach told me to do. It is a team effort; we all win or we all lose."

"So what do you play in orchestra?"

"The violin, my mom insisted I learned how to play it since she played it. It was good eye, hand coordination. It helped my baseball catching. I always thought what came next in the piece. It made me more aware, something about discipline that carried over into other areas of our lives. I sound just like Mr. Topps, our orchestra leader. His daily preaching is a given. And you know if it weren't for the violin, I guess that I would never even see my mom."

"Well, I never see mine. We left her back in New Mexico with the desert and the cactus. My dad said that in a marriage people sometimes change at the same time or at different times. My mom, a New Mexico rock, refused to change so the three of us just left. One school is really just as good as another. But a mother is one of a kind. Missing her, destroyed me. You would think that she cared but doesn't."

"Sarah, I just bet that you're going to make a lot of friends here. Me for instance, would you like to be friends?"

Sarah gazed at me intently. I was positive that she would say no. Embarrassed, I wanted in the worst way to take my offer back. But before I could, Sarah nodded her head.

"The more I talk to you, the better I like you. Yes, friends then." The bus stopped abruptly and my so called casual friends made faces at me. My face flushed. I didn't want Sarah to see them.

"Tomorrow, Sarah."

Before my feet hit the ground. "Hey CJ what happened to you? It's all over the school. Did you ever go to the hospital and there was something about your dad?"

These friends were just curious and didn't really care. Not close buddies, they had no baseball flowing through their veins. Those who cared already knew. They couldn't wait until Monday. Hurrying, I didn't want to be late to class. The girls that I liked thought lateness was very rude.

There was a target, dead ahead of me. My feet were lead and everything stopped. The most beautiful girl in the world stopped and turned and waited. I forced myself to breathe and made myself walk and talk.

"BJ, I never had a chance to thank you for what you did for me. But once you revived me nothing was right. My dad was in the hospital and I had to get to him."

Her soft tinted brown hair swished across her face. "I'm just glad that I could help you. It was nice being up close and personal with you if you know what I mean." Then she laughed a carefree laugh that made the whole world better. Her warmth seeped through me, flames from a kindled fire on a bitter cold day. Without stopping for a breath, I told BJ all about my unnerving weekend. Eyes attached to mine, she listened.

"Things happen and we don't always know why. Your dad will heal but it will take some time and lots of patience. Are you prepared for what it takes?"

The question didn't need an answer. At lunch, we shared sandwiches and pickles outside at a stone wall table just for two. We talked non-stop. BJ never had a brother and always wanted one. I hoped that I wouldn't fill that longing. I told BJ about my plans to get a job so that I could help out at home. By tomorrow, she assured me I would have one. Not only was BJ beautiful on the outside but more so on the inside where it really counted. At that very moment my heart was captured never again to be the same. How could BJ be so sure about everything? I mean it wasn't like she had a manual to study. Abruptly getting up, her eyes said tomorrow.

AN INTERN

Bj insisted I meet her dad. He unnerved me. My hair was surely messed up and all over the place since I rode my bike over to the college. She just told me where, when and nothing else. It all seemed so secret so covert, so sudden. Maybe he was a spy, a military spy. His office was a war zone: boxes piled on top of one another, a small cluttered desk in the middle of the room, a disconnected telephone just waiting to be plugged in, and books everywhere crammed in every spot possible.

BJ's father was tall, very tall and very skinny. His legs were so long by the time you got up to his face you were tired. A seasoned risk taker, maybe his younger risks did him in. His eyes darted all around the room and finally landed on me.

"Son, please sit down and be comfortable."

"Sir, where shall I sit?"

"Any box will do. Sir isn't necessary, it's Henry. Upfront, I want you to know that I love my daughters more than life itself and would do anything in the world for them. BJ told me that you needed a job. Am I right about that?"

"Yes, we need the money. It's because of my dad. He was injured and probably will be out of work for quite a while. Who knows if he will ever be able to return? So somehow I will have to fill his shoes."

I turned my head. Men were not supposed to cry. And now I was a man.

"BJ also told me something about a baseball mitt. That you always sleep with it. Is that right?"

"Yes, that's right."

"Great, you can start right now. All the boxes need to be unloaded and the contents need to be labeled and organized. I am not an organizer but BJ told me that you were." He smiled; a warm smile that crept across the room. His eyes twinkled like you know who and it wasn't even Christmas.

BJ was so lucky to have a healthy dad who could see, move, and speak clearly. Did she know it? Never again would I take anyone for granted.

Tomorrow, I would start fixing my own dad. The eye exercises would not fail. There was so much to tell him. Bj refused to leave my mind. Maybe dad could tell me how to talk to BJ, to make her wonder about me the way I wondered about her.

After a few hours of hard labor, my back ached more than my arms. Just in the nick of time Henry pointed to his watch and from the open window I heard the fading cry of a steam whistle from a passing train.

"CJ you need to pace yourself son, the boxes aren't going anywhere. Oh and a little advice about my daughter; don't let her rattle you. She acts like she's twenty even though she's twelve. Most women are like that son. Just be yourself." Being a man was complicated: a job, a girl, and getting along with her father who sort of liked me.

Once I got home my good feelings and confidence vanished. Things were back in boxes. Mother was asleep on the sofa and everything was strewn around the house. Loneliness latched onto me and shoved me down. Covering mother with a blanket, I knew that it was my turn to take care of her. All that I ever heard from my friends was how beautiful mother was: her face, her hair, her perfect figure. They were all secretly in love with her. Since I hardly saw her I wasn't. Mother looked beyond me. I wasn't even there.

"Guess what mother? I found a job, a real job at the college. I couldn't wait to tell you."

"Do you really think that it matters? Will it bring your father home?"

"It might; it just might."

"He can't see, he can barely move. And if he ever gets out, his job will not be there waiting." Fear spoke. I refused to listen.

"I can't change the horrible accident, but I can change how we react to it." Even if I messed everything up, hope dragged me forward. Late into the night, tomorrow consumed me. The eye drills, the index cards,

I knew them by heart. Tomorrow Dad was going to see or I would know the reason why.

School was a blur; my mind was attached to my mission. Riding my bike to the hospital, my legs complained and were ignored. Today, I needed both my Dad's undivided attention, his full concentration and my own. Expecting me, Dad and his bound-up right leg was hoisted up ready to pop the pulley.

"CJ, I was certain that you would be here today after school. For the last twenty-four hours I have thought of little else. Your mother just stared and cried. But the two of us man to man, we will . . . Dad stopped.

"Yes, Dad, we will. Right now, you need to think of me as your teacher. I was ready, prepared and did my homework. I wanted him to slowly open up his eyes as much as he could. Struggling, my dad finally gave up.

"Son, it won't work; they just won't listen to me."

"Dad, remember that day when you told me to see the ball falling in my glove even though my eyes were closed? Well now it's your turn. I want you to see your eyes opened."

Beautiful pictures of the National Parks and Hawaii were carefully taped on my index cards. Using every descriptive word that I ever heard, I lured my dad in like a big fish. My dad had to see these pictures. Frustrated, his ears hurt from all of the concentration. His eyes jumped in and opened. Seeing, he caught the ball.

"Son, they are blurry but I can see them."

"Dad, look at my face. Do you remember? Focus on it."

My dad's eyes squinted uncomfortably and then suddenly locked on to my eyes. Sobbing, he pulled me to his chest.

"Your face was the only thing that I had to see. I couldn't go another day without seeing my son."

My dad held me close for eternity. The first part of my mission was successful. Every day we would do a little more. This world had completely worn me out. Exhausted, my dad and I fell into one another's love.

A professional, frustrated cry reached my ears. "Visiting hours are over; you can't be in here."

"We are not visiting. We are training. Dad show her what we have done."

The nurse placed my dad's dinner tray in front of him and started cutting up his food.

"That won't be necessary; I can do it myself." Well, the baffled nurse almost fell off her chair as she watched my dad prepare and feed himself without any assistance.

"But your chart stated that you couldn't see."

"The chart is incorrect. You need to change it."

All bases loaded, my dad just hit a homerun. We flashed one another one of those triumphant baseball smiles; I then knew that together dad and I would play this game victoriously.

THE CONCERT

With dad seeing his way, my mind was freed up. Suddenly I realized that the orchestra hadn't been part of my week. Neglected, my violin stayed in its case and never complained. When I tuned it up, it let me know. Moaning and groaning every string revolted. After numerous apologies, my violin finally sounded the way it should. Never again would I abandon it.

At school, Mr. Finny, the orchestra leader, cordoned me off in the hallway. "CJ, I know that recently life has piled up on you. Our concert is next Saturday. Do you still want to play that solo?" If I had false teeth, they would have popped out.

"Mr. Finny, I forgot, you know my dad and everything else. I mean if my head were not attached . . ." But it was. Mr. Finny's musical eyes twinkled.

"Then I will expect you on that stage at 7:00 sharp ready to woo the audience with your prepared strings."

A good part of my heart sank. Always up front, dead center, my parents sat and filled me with the confidence and calmness that I required. Dad's empty seat had to be filled. None of my baseball buddies would ever sit through an hour of classical music, not even tied down. The answer called from down the hall.

"CJ, I just had to talk to you. The job, did you like him, you know my dad? Did you have to do a lot of work? Did he even let you rest? My dad said he would be hard on you." My mind jumped back two days. Should I tell BJ? No she should squirm a little.

"You know I don't think your dad liked me at all." A gusty storm blew over BJ's face. "Your dad doesn't like me, he loves me." Instantly, BJ grabbed my hand.

"I knew it; I just knew it. How could he not love you?"

My heart burned inside me. How could I ask her? I mean what if she said no?

Sometimes a man has to do what he has to do.

"BJ, there is something that I just have to know. Next Saturday there is an orchestra performance and, well, maybe if you are free . . . My eyes hit the floor.

"Yes, but only if you are in it." How good that one word sounded; it changed everything. My mother and my girl would now sit side by side.

Working three days a week after school and spending every other spare minute that I had at the hospital left little time for practicing. But every night my violin and I fell into one another's arms. My solo piece became me. I lived it, breathed it and dreamed it. Mother seemed okay with sharing the lime light with BJ. I just told her that BJ wanted to play the violin. Mother would never know how I really felt; it was forbidden. She just assumed that baseball was my first and only love. That's how I wanted it.

Saturday got tired of waiting and finally showed up. For the occasion, mother surprised me with a Polo shirt that glowed in the dark, a spectacular red and blue stripped tie, and brand new beige leather loafers. Tan kakis, a uniform's must completed the outfit.

My chestnut colored violin glowed as well. For an hour I saturated it with lemon oil and buffed, wanting those highlights to light up. They did, as well as ready formed blisters.

Distracting my mind, I pretended it was just another Saturday. But it wasn't and the moment arrived. Up on stage, everything shrank back except my two supporters whose cheering jumped out of the crowd. Mother was especially elegant and BJ matched her, makeup for makeup and dress for dress. A proud peacock, my feathers puffed up.

Once my solo was announced, an aching pit stuck in my stomach. Reality charged right at me. No mixing and matching could stop it. Dad wasn't here. Then I heard his voice whisper, "Make those strings sing," my dad's way of saying you are prepared so bring it. Blocking everything out, I played with my spirit instead of my mind. The bow became alive and each string obeyed. Opening my eyes I stared at love, a mother's love and a girl's love. Both were here for me.

Half way through the piece, the tempo changed and that's when I heard it. One of the strings just popped. Screeching to a halt, I was an eighteen wheeler. A feverish cry echoed down one row through another. Steam rose from the over-worked string. Then an amazing thing happened. Mr. Finney walked up on stage and handed me his violin. No one was even allowed to breathe on it. Mr. Finney was an accomplished violinist; he was even famous for playing gigs on television. He trusted me with his instrument; that one thought blew me into another dimension.

A hush enveloped the auditorium. Everyone just held their breath. BJ started clapping softly and everyone followed suit. When I touched those professional strings, the fog of fear disappeared. It was as if Mr. Finney and I finished the solo together. It was a defining moment for me knowing that I could do anything regardless of what happened around me.

When I finished, the crowd exploded. My mother looked as if she were going to run up on the stage and kiss me. Horrified, I quickly shook my head side to side; she stopped and sat back down. If BJ had that same look it would have been awesome and the kiss of the century would be on tomorrow's front page.

Funny, my spotlight stage time was over but now I was more nervous than ever. Mr. Finney's prize violin was still out of its case and entrusted to me. What if I dropped it? What if I banged into something?

My mind was a slowed down skateboard and quickly halted as our orchestra played a few favorites together. The other chaired violinists made extra room for me. No one wanted to be near that violin.

Mr. Finney radiated pride as we played almost flawlessly. Before I knew it, the audience stood up and roared. I thought maybe someone important had entered, like the queen or president. No, it was just for us. Nothing could top the glow of that night or so I thought. But when BJ grabbed my hand and wouldn't let go, I promised never to wash my hand again.

Mother did her best to stifle it, but my heart was abducted. The three of us walked hand in hand with Mr. Finney's violin. Dad was right with us and I heard him say, 'That's my son,' and I knew that I would always be his son, no matter what.

WORKING DAD OUT

M y abducted heart pedaled even faster. I wanted to be the first to tell dad all about my night of fame. Chuckling to myself I could still see preoccupied Mr. Finney on our doorstep this morning at 6:00 a.m. It wasn't for breakfast. His prized violin was safely tucked away in my case and mine in his. When we exchanged violins, I could almost hear a triumphant bugle sounding afar off. Suppressed tears of joy streaked across Mr. Finney's face. His heart was abducted by a violin.

Reaching the hospital, I almost ran non-stop to the elevator. Rushing into Dad's room, I noticed right away that his tortured leg was no longer in traction. A ripened papaya, I burst open.

"Dad, I did it. The solo was like gooey, never ending syrup that just poured out of me." Adding a bit more than really happened, I just wanted my dad to be there and he was. His eyes lit up with fatherly pride bursting all of his buttons.

Consumed with BJ I asked, "Dad, tell me about you and mom, about the first time when you held hands." He couldn't remember. Life tore their hands apart.

"You know, son, it was just too long ago. But you look like you can't wait to tell me something so what is it? Has baseball been replaced as a first in your life? It might just happen one of these days."

"Dad, I felt sick and scared and warm and wonderful, a rainbow of feelings rushed through me. It was different than our love; it was my own love. When I am with her my mind is like one of our clogged-up sinks. Nothing works right and my words don't make any sense."

"That's the way it works, son. Girls, women just make us weak; that's why you have to be prepared and ready for it."

"Does it ever stop?"

"Yes, but it takes intervention. Your words need to be the ones to make her feel important. So you have to find out everything you can about what she likes and become an expert on it."

"So I need to impress her with what I know?"

"Yes, something like that." Why were girls so complicated when we were so simple? I wondered if my dad ever impressed my mom. Maybe when you were married for a long time, you no longer needed to be an expert. There was a deepening sadness about my dad. Then and there I decided never to bring up the subject again.

The exercises commenced: Dad's hands squeezed soft rubber balls, his arms pulled back and forth on an attached wall bar, but his legs refused to budge.

"Dad, it's all about upper body strength so when you do start moving your legs will get some help. The repeated exercises were done in sequence, over and over again. Suddenly dad collapsed and fell back into his bed. A throat cleared.

"Your dad is not a teenager nor will he ever be one again." It was the floor nurse, an angel dressed all in white with her white cap pinned to her dark curly tucked under hair.

"You need to take it easy on him. But I am glad to see you worked him out; no one else does. He will be up in that chair tomorrow. I just know it." Dad was in beautiful, professional hands, much better than mine.

"Tomorrow, we will start again tomorrow."

Hungry, dad looked as if he were more than ready for his meatloaf dinner and attention from this beautiful young nurse. That's the dad that I knew and loved. Overwhelmed, I knew my dad was given back to me.

But I didn't let up on dad all week. Each day I pressed him beyond his limit. The payoff came on Saturday when we walked down the hall with his walker. A victory of firsts, I was keenly aware that dad was mending and that meant coming home.

The conversation from the lounge echoed down the hall.   "I don't know why that kid tries so hard; it isn't like his father is ever going to be right again. Why doesn't somebody just tell him the truth?"

Anger and resentment choked me. While Dad rested down the hall, I couldn't get to the lounge fast enough.

"Hey, did you have something that you wanted to tell me?"

"No, kid, only that I wish I had a son like you." A wisp of their former selves, both of the shriveled-up men were confined to wheel chairs. My anger and resentment vanished as weakened hands grabbed my hands and held on tightly. Tears pressed against my eyes as I promised both men that my dad and I were going to play baseball once again. In disbelief, they both stared at me and then asked if they too could bring their mitts.

That night mother and I had a much needed, a long over- due conversation about dad.

"Mother, dad walked today, I mean really walked."

"I know the head nurse called me and informed me about his progress. CJ, you know what that means don't you? It isn't that your dad is going back to work any time soon. It may take months of recovery maybe even a year. His health insurance will cover some of the costs but not all. Your job will help, well both of our jobs will help."

"Mom, you got a job? But you said you would never go to work."

"Well, it's not like a desk job or anything. It's part time work, a few hours here and there, and it's simple. I walked in; they shook my hand and never let it go. It is about showing products on television. Only my hands are seen; nothing else. It isn't about what I wear; I don't even have to get dressed up or get my hair done. So you see my hands are becoming famous. I called some health care services about possible help here at home for your father. But their rates are astronomical."

"Mom, don't worry. I will ask around and see what I can find out."

"Just like your father always wanting to take care of everything. You remind me so much of him always on the move."

The next day after school, the boxes at work seemed to get heavier and heavier. Discouraged, I sat down and just started scribbling on a pad of paper.

Last night's conversation seeped into my mind. BJ's father noticed the change in me.

"Troubled, son? Sometimes when you talk it out, it helps." So I talked it out. It was probably way more than he wanted to hear.

"You know it just sounds to me like you need to find a nurses' aide and I just happen to know one who needs a job. I'll be right back."

Within minutes, he returned with the biggest smile.

"It's all settled then; Mort is available and ready to give up his gym job."

"His gym job?"

"Yes, that's how he stays in shape so he can do all of that heavy lifting and bathing and care-giving."

"CJ, I will dock your wages to cover Mort's salary and that should do it. He can start any time. Don't let him scare you. With all of his tattoo markings he could pass for a newspaper's front page. But it was fallout from the war. He's a Vietnam Veteran and more than able to take care of your dad."

There was a two beat knock on the door, code-like, then a pause and again a two beat knock. I quickly went into the adjoining room. One professor at a time was all that I could handle.

The conversation seeped through the wall. "Dad, Sis is just boy crazy and I couldn't listen to any more of it. I wish there were no such things as boys; they are just a bunch of trouble and just wear you out. His name is all over her notebooks. Obsessive, can't you stop it, dad?"

"Young lady, weren't you telling me just the other day that you met an interesting young man on the bus?"

"Yes, but I haven't thought twice about him. I haven't seen him since. He probably already moved. But you know, Dad, I really liked him and he seemed to really like me. He was different I just knew that he loved his dad the way that I loved you." The voice sounded so familiar. But one little girl sounded just like another. I needed to find out who belonged to the voice.

"Sir, I am sorry to interrupt but where do I . . . And there was Sarah the young precocious girl that I met on the bus. As if stricken, Sarah shrieked and ran out of the room. "Sir, Sarah is your daughter?"

"You certainly seem to get around. Did you have to captivate both of my girls?" With a twinkle in his eye Herald looked as if was transported back to seventh grade. I hoped he didn't get stuck there.

"I never intended any of this to happen. You have to believe me. Sarah was just so different, so confident and I needed a seat on that bus. Now it fits together, because both of your daughters just wanted to talk about you."

"CJ, I remember that seventh grade seemed so grown-up. Just take it easy on my girls. Okay?" It was more than okay. My poor brain could hardly handle BJ, who without even trying captured me and never even knew it.

THE DECEPTION

D ad seemed very pleased that his boss visited him, bearing good tidings of encouraging words. Both enjoyed a long conversation about the business and where it was headed. Having won prized insurance salesman of the year many times, dad was eager to return and do it again. Happy for dad, I too was encouraged. Maybe my life's earnings wouldn't all go to Mort. A few steps behind me, mother closed in on us.

The head nurse was more like a bothered mother hen and flapped her wings glad to finally get us all together. "Your husband no longer needs this bed. He needs his own bed and loving care at home. Healing takes time and progresses at its' own rate. Mrs. Moore, thanks to your son's creativity, our patient here has healed much quicker than anyone possibly thought."

A fog of horror crossed my mother's face. Temporarily losing her balance, mother collapsed in the nearby chair. "Mrs. Moore, I just know that you can handle this." Some of head nurses' fallen feathers shed as she departed quickly down the hall.

"But we aren't ready. There's no one to take care of you. CJ and I couldn't possibly lift, dress, and provide for you."

"Well, then I guess I will just have to find a new home."

"No wait," I was a launched rocket and burst into the conversation. My boss, Mr. Thorpe took care of everything; it's Mort the walking newspaper. He is an aide, on standby, just waiting for the call."

Perplexed, my mother grabbed, hugged, and squeezed the very life out of me then passed me to my dad. Funny when I pitched in to help, my parents were shocked as if I couldn't possibly be their son. Pride rose up. At least for one more night I was still man of the house.

Too bright and too early Mort showed up. Sputtering and heaving, his old jalopy announced his arrival. Bags of groceries were tucked under his arms and a big grin pasted on his face. Eagerly I waited to get a look at his infamous tattoos.

Right from the start, Mort took over, cooked breakfast, scrambled eggs and bacon, honey-dipped toast, and fresh orange juice which he squeezed himself. He only ate fresh prepared food with no additives.

Mort told us more than we wanted to know: his war days as a soldier, his coach days at the gym, and his lonely days as a by-gone father. He had lost track of his two sons and had no idea where they were. Mort didn't believe in love but was loving. His ex-wife hated him because he abandoned her for his cars, entering race after race, but never won. Allergic, his sons wanted nothing to do with his cars. The oil laced air gagged them. They had no desire for finger nails that resembled a garage mechanic's. In the end Mort lost everything that meant anything. His tattoos revealed his emptiness.

Opening the door for mother, Mort instructed us where to sit. Mother looked like a school girl: waited on and being told what to do. Mort could tell me anything and I listened. He needed a pair of ears to hear him; the way we needed a pair of hands to help us. His war stories were gruesome, the more vivid the better he liked them. Quite by accident Mort started caring for the wounded. Overseas, they needed an army medic and he became one.

Instinctively. Mort had a heavy foot. Holding her breath, mother just closed her eyes. My eyes were hyper- extended.

"Mort, we have the whole day to get to the hospital." I quipped. Mort laughed as if he had forgotten how.

"Pretty good kid." With some of his chipped, broken teeth showcased, he gave me one of those confident grins.

"Mort, slow down my dad needs me."

"I wouldn't know what that's like. No one has ever needed me, certainly not my family, maybe a few car rodeo girls. The war trained me not to care, not to feel."

"Well, you're not in the war any more. We need you." Mort pulled the car over to the side of the road and stopped. With tear-streaked eyes, he turned around, and hugged me.

"Thank you, son." At that moment, I became exactly that. Mort missed his sons terribly, so I became a fill-in. Mort actually slowed down some but mother never took her hand off the door handle as if considering her options. The hazardous driving shocked us. By the time we got to the hospital our driving etiquette was altered forever.

Dad was ready, dressed, packed, and seated. As if a pile of socks, Mort picked dad up out of his chair and placed him exactly center in the wheel chair. Dad breathed a huge sigh of relief.

"You're hired." Oddly, everyone was drawn to Mort. Before we got home, Dad and he were inseparable. It was a good thing since Mort was not to leave his side except to sleep.

Mother was quiet, maybe too quiet. Seated next to me she was in her own distant world. Etched in my mother's face was the strain of the last two months: every day, every hour, and every minute. Her face told its story. No longer self-absorbed, mother had to change. Searching frantically for her old lifestyle was a complete waste of time; that husband, that salesman, that provider, was gone forever. In his place, was a frail, dependent, beaten man whom she hardly recognized. Care was what he needed and care wasn't anything that she knew how to give.

Before the accident my father traveled constantly, empty weeks and weekends was the norm without a word from him. Filled with shopping, friends, and idle chatter mother's life evolved with me as the center. My friends entertained her and she thrived on compliments from middle school kids. The accident roughly jammed our lives back together again.

Dad was thrilled to be home.

"CJ, is my room ready? Have you thought that far ahead?"

"Dad, just the way you left it, except for a few changes. Mort's got a pull out bed next to yours just in case you need to get up in the night. Mom and I will change it up a bit and stay in the bunk room. It should b e a lot of fun, just like camp."

As soon as we reached our street, Mort sprang into action. He was the commander in chief of this operation. "Leave your dad to me; that's why I'm here." And sure enough Mort got dad fed, tucked in and found a new set of ears for his war stories.

Disappearing, mother couldn't get to her bedroom fast enough. Something was wrong. Where was the celebration? Empty love wafted around the house. My love celebrated. Wanting to be alone with my dad, I closed the door and sat by his bed.

"Dad, don't worry. It's just going to take some readjusting."

"Son, as long as I have you, that's all that I need. Your mother and I just need a little time."

Mother's whimpering went through the wall. Mort heard it and turned up the radio. One broken heart at a time was all he could handle.

Slowly the house quieted down. Restless I spent most of the night making sure that mother slept.

Waking up with the sun, I couldn't help but hear my father's cries: The door was jammed and I couldn't get in.

'Dad, what's wrong?" Frantic, I couldn't find Mort anywhere. Dad yelled something about a letter, a liar, and that he needed a home not a shelter. Hurtling myself against the door, it opened.

The very first thing that dad didn't need to see was in his hands. Once I pried it loose, the ink smudged. The letter arrived late yesterday afternoon by Federal Express so we assumed it was a welcome home letter. It welcomed unemployment: short, precise, and to the point. There was no need for dad to hurry back. Regrettably his position was filled.

"But how could he lie to my face?" Dad sobbed.

"Dad, maybe he just didn't have the guts to tell you." The front door slammed and Mort ran in, red faced, sweaty, and embarrassed.

"In the morning, I run three miles. When I left, he was fast asleep. What happened?"

After around the bed discussion, the letter's contents were dismissed and never brought up again. Mort insisted dad take some sleeping medication that knocked him out. Ripping up the letter, Mort's anger raged as if his own life was on it. His insides burned and all he saw was his ex-wife's indifference, the divorce decree.

THE DANCE THAT NEVER WAS

The weekend was heavy on my mind. Well suited armor cracked, raw emotions were sewage that seeped out. Circumstances did their best to destroy our family. For once, I was glad to be back in school.

Rumors winged around the school. Our baseball team was out of the running for the state finals. Both coaches were kicked out of the runoffs for unruly behavior. Kids were angry and out of hand. A group of my buddies, heralded baseball players, pelted the coach's old ford mustang with rotten eggs. The school's secretary's phone never stopped. All day long, two by two like in Noah's day, parents stormed down the hall towards the principal's office demanding explanations. It was the first and only time that I actually felt anything for the principal. Today he earned his salary.

Exhausted from my own family drama, nothing really fazed me until I heard her voice; then I was a running greyhound with perked ears.

"CJ there is a dance after school next Friday, just for us the seventh graders. Do you think, I mean would you like to, well, meet me there?" I hesitated. A dance with a girl, the only girl that mattered besides my mother. It was way too dangerous.

"Sure that sounds great," I heard my mouth reply. I would have to start memorizing questions to ask her, the left-over index cards would do. BJ loved baseball maybe even more than I did. Batting averages on the pros would have to be studied. This would really be my chance to impress BJ.

Throughout the whole school, the same question reverberated. Who asked whom? The cool kids were always asked first by the girls. The leftovers then had to gravel and ask the remaining girls. You just didn't want to have to ask a girl anything for fear she would laugh, ridicule, and ruin you forever. In a matter of seconds you fell from cool to frigid. Then you might as well transfer to another school. Your name meant nothing.

Days passed but the best part of each day was what happened after school. The park became our hangout. Mort did wheelies with dad in the chair. Right before my very eyes, two grown men became kids again. The light danced in each of us. There was an unaccustomed freedom in the park. Nobody told us what we could or couldn't do, who we could or couldn't be. There was no one to please. Little kids brushed by my dad wanting to know why he was in a wheel chair. His stories got better and better; eyes opened wider and wider. There was just something about a place with no walls.

"Son, you need to make a list of what you couldn't possibly do without. I mean knowing how we stand and all."

"I don't need a list. It's you and probably mom. The rest means little to me."

"So the clothes, the jeans, the sneakers, the house, the car, all of it; your world as you know it could end quite suddenly without any backup. If it were to happen that way, you need to be prepared."

"Dad, I could live with you in a tent with Mort's help and be happy."

That was all that he needed to hear. "But your baseball, your big dreams."

"Dad, your accident taught me what I needed to know. Today is what I live for not yesterday or tomorrow." My dad glowed like embers of a forgotten fire.

"Dad, there is something that I just have to know. You and mom never taught me how to dance. I probably just never watched both of you on the dance floor."

Dad jerked his face around, "Dance, no there was never a dance. There never seemed to be time. If there had been a dance, just one dance, maybe things would be different."

Overhearing, Mort remembered when he was thirteen. CJ needed the moves. Mort turned up the tunes. He never left the house without his portable CD player; his musical back pack. Mort was a rubber band and sprang back and forth all over that park. Other Kids joined in. Before long, we danced in a circle all around my dad. Mort pulled him up out of the chair and rocked him back and forth. It was a dance that I will never forget.

For a brief moment, my dad forgot the terror, the pain, the fear, the doubt, and the heartache. There were no limitations. Then Mort grabbed me and twirled me around. Before I got dizzy he taught me how to move and steer someone else at the same time. We practiced every day for two weeks. Becoming a family affair, I was more than ready for the dance.

The big day finally arrived It had been the longest two weeks of my teenage life. Mother bought me a new red plaid polo shirt, grey pleated pants, and the coolest light grey leather loafers. Mother encouraged my good looks.

So there I was at school, packed full of prepared questions and baseball averages, all dressed up with nowhere to go. BJ was gone. No one had seen her all day. Each class came and went. Any moment I just knew that she would barge through a door; but she never did.

I was the talk of the school and everyone added their own version. The word was that BJ set me up and had no intention of going with me to the dance.

My heart gave way. Opening my locker, I took the carefully wrapped scented corsage and handed it to the closest girl that I could find. I scuffed up my loafers and tussled my hair.

My so-called friends insisted that I go to the dance anyway, so I did just for spite. My name meant something to me and I could get any girl in that school and I did. Never before had I even looked at the other girls. I didn't take my eyes off of them. They all looked identical, just like their mothers, dolls with heavy makeup, tight jeans, low tops; clothes that didn't really fit. When they opened up their mouths, any possibility scooted out the door. Boring was too good of a word to describe what they had to say. They didn't think, didn't care, and didn't mind a bit that I knew it.

No one wanted to dance so the teachers initiated it. Pulling us up out of the bleachers, they paired us together indiscriminately. The music was better than Mort's tapes. There was a DJ with long braided hair with cool tunes. He cracked joke after joke. There was no pressure. Everyone laughed at him instead of one another. There were line dances and everyone just hung on to the person in front of them and someone started the Bunny hop. Can you imagine? We probably looked like third graders but it was so much fun. Just when I started to breathe, to enjoy; there she was by the door. With Smudged tears, BJ forced herself to look at me.

"I just didn't want you to hate me, to leave you this way. My dad received a certified notice that my mother wants custody and a divorce. I guess that was her plan all along and why she wouldn't even consider moving here. According to my dad, we are not for sale. So we are officially on the run.

All day long, we packed boxes of stuff and left behind what wouldn't fit in the car." BJ's presence stole the moment. Every eye was on us, students and teachers alike. Privacy was allusive. Almost tripping over myself, I led BJ outside. Grabbing BJ's hand, I pulled her next to me. BJ's face was a magnet and headed for mine. I turned my head away. Shame burst through.

"Very sorry, I just wanted to kiss you goodbye." Embarrassed beyond words, BJ turned and ran. Now, not only was I branded as stood up but also marked a coward. My mind reeled.

Reluctantly, I walked back inside the gymnasium and grabbed the closest teacher to me leading her to the dance floor. Steering her closer, I went in for the kiss and was rudely slapped and pushed away. I knew that I would be suspended for weeks, maybe the rest of the year but I didn't care. Now there was really something to talk about. None of it mattered. The only one that meant anything to me was taken away without my permission.

COMMUNITY SERVICE

My gutsy inappropriate behavior at school was reprimanded with gutsy leadership. They decided to put my advances to good use. I was put in charge of the outreach committee.

In Social Studies, Mr. Bindler showed us a documentary film photographed in Africa where the children had no shoes, few clothes, and walked in the garbage mounds looking for food. Many were orphaned and in need of medical attention. Hook worms were in their feet.

Visibly sickened, some of the weaker girls in our class ran out of the room never making it to the restroom. Graphic and scary, I quickly forget the abscessed knot in my stomach since BJ's sudden departure. As a group of spoiled, well fed and fashion- minded kids, we decided to get involved and change it. Mr. Binder appointed me chairman giving me the task of setting up individual groups that came up with intervention plans.

Paired together, the cool kids and the nerds were unaccustomed to even looking at one another. Away from their friends, the cool kids shut down. The nerds got them talking. Before you knew it, creative individuals blossomed. Each committee was responsible for devising ways to raise money for the struggling orphans. Bake sales, sneaker donations, rummage sales with donated clothes were some of the suggestions. But we needed something big, something that the whole community could get involved in. One of the nerd's fathers owned a restaurant in town.

A student directed dinner for the community sparked an avalanche of interest and before we knew it phone calls were made. Permission was granted to host an Italian extravaganza next Saturday night at Mitch's with all proceeds going to the outreach. One of the cool kid's dad was a reporter and he agreed to do a story advertising the dinner and the demise of the African children. Their cries would be heard.

Overnight kids became waiters, greeters, and cooks. Volunteering, our very own teachers trained us how to talk, walk, and carry trays properly. But our teachers didn't cook. So the mothers jumped in and flooded us with recipes for sauces and everything Italian. As it turned out, the mothers were put in charge of anything that entered and left that kitchen, including us.

In preparation, Invisible do's and dont's lost their footing. Right before my very eyes, our teachers changed into real people. After school, guitars and voices blended together. Hard at work, the teachers created musical encantadas that would be performed at the extravaganza. For me, it was difficult to even consider that a teacher did anything but teach. Teachers were part of the school, rooted plants without any other possibility. They never retired and never left, never wanted to do anything but stay in the pot.

Even in the grocery store, I avoided all possible contact and quickly changed aisles if spotted. Randomly talking to me or my mother was a recurrent nightmare. Who knew what would come out of one potted plant?

Even the art teacher contributed and designed invitations and printed them out on special glossy paper. Everything was going smoothly until we hit a glitch, what to wear?

The girls didn't want to look like the boys and the boys didn't care what they looked like. Since it was a community project and ultimately the teachers were responsible: black pants, white shirts, and optional sneakers were the designated uniform. Hair needed to be neat and out of our face. That would be harder for the boys than the girls.

A few days before the fundraiser, we were given permission to decorate at Mitch's which was transformed into a little Africa. Murals of animals, hunters, and huts were all over the walls. In shop class, some of the kids constructed wooden canoes which greeted you at the door. The teachers drew straws and the one who lost got to sit in it serenading guest after guest as he paddled into the Amazon.

Before I knew it, I stirred away, tasting, adding dabs of this and that just like a professional chef. Chip and I were both given big white chef hats and short white coats. If the food were cold or awful, I guess they wanted to know who to blame. The stove was really hot and there wasn't enough room for four cooks. The two spirited mothers chirped away in Italian and hummed love songs under their breath. Their instructions were followed to the tee. Chip and I both breathed a huge sigh of relief. Neither one of us had ever stirred a pot.

Calm preparation was a peering owl that hooted and flew out the door when everyone suddenly arrived all at once. Nerves rattled, tongues tied, and mistakes glowed. Almost every guest had selected a favorite table and no one could convince them otherwise. The tables looked professionally decorated with beige and gold tablecloths and unique desert-looking flowers. Gold glitter was sprinkled throughout the carpet. Beauty and impatience came toe to toe. Rescuing the young hostess, Ms. Barnes, a teacher, instructed the disorderly bunch that they would be seated in an orderly fashion. Only a teacher could do that and get away with it.

According to Mr. Binder, regardless of what the guest said or did, the guest was always right. It was as if you had a hundred parents and were expected to please all of them at the same time. For once, I was thankful that I was in the kitchen with piled plates of spaghetti and garlic bread. Mrs. Bennin brought fresh herbs, Rosemary and Thyme, from her garden. She must have given them special names for the special occasion. Very canned, very salty sardines were added to the sauce. You would expect sardines on the end of a fishing line not swimming in your spaghetti sauce.

Even for one night, I never realized how difficult it was to work in a restaurant. I would never again give a waiter a hard time. When guests were hungry, the food better be hot, ready, and awfully good. It must have been because plates kept coming back wanting more. Thank goodness mothers planned and looked head. Ready and prepared for the onslaught, the two Italian cooks brought their own specialties. Out of nowhere, vats of covered sauce and spaghetti appeared. Seconds were an after-thought.

Unexpectedly, Mother arrived with an escort. Witty and comical, he pulled the tables together and told off color jokes. He was the center of attention. Everyone wondered if he were a distant uncle? An uncle, covered with tattoos, comically dressed, and using words that some had never heard? Then I relaxed; it was just Mort. I was so glad he was here joining them, I inhaled a huge plate of spaghetti. With her casual quietness,

Mother reminded me that the food wasn't going anywhere. After all I wasn't in Africa.

Just like the guests arrived, they departed as a flock of geese with one big flurry of movement. Everyone took a deep breath including all four cooks. Then I heard it.

"The fire, the kitchen, the stove, everything was going to burn." It was the worst smell, the burnt odor of a major mistake. Then I saw a crazed fog, billowing black smoke that poured out of the kitchen. Thankfully most guests were gone but those who remained jumped up as if they were already lit up.

Mother insisted that I leave with them but I just couldn't. My pride refused. I was one of the cooks; it was our kitchen, our responsibility. Within minutes screeching sirens flooded the street followed by a brighter than red fire engine.

"Boys, stand back. You don't want to breathe this or get it on you. A volcanic eruption of water flooded the kitchen followed by white gooey muck that was sprayed all over the stove and appliances. A grease fire was the worst kind.

Chip read my frantic mind. "You know they will sue you and me for everything that we have, jeans, tennis shoes, cool shirts, your violin and what our families own. We might as well board a plane for Africa while we still can. Tomorrow will be too late. Blending in with those unfortunate kids, we will become part of the scenery. No one would be able to tell the difference." Chip's words stung my heart. Maybe he was right.

As we hung our dejected heads, the teachers huddled together in a violated group knowing that ultimately they were responsible. Mr. Bindler was devastated but came up with a plan: clean it all up and that was exactly what we did. After all the fireman had saved the restaurant; it just smelled awful and looked ghastly with blackened muck right out of a swamp.

But out of nowhere, people started arriving with all kinds of cleaning equipment. With their protective outerwear, professional cleaners shooed us out of the way. No one had deserted us; on the contrary working cheerleaders rallied around us.

Inadvertently even the uninformed public got involved . . . Television reporters arrived swinging their cameras in our direction and wanted the cooks' interviews. We cried out for support and the money poured in like a maladjusted hurricane. Mr. Binder's face charged into a teacher's pride as he pounded us on our backs for keeping calm in a desperate situation. Chip and I broke into uncontrolled laughter knowing full well that our African plane tickets were no longer needed. A disaster turned into an overflowing blessing.

At home the celebrity status didn't change. Envelopes kept emptying out into the room through the slot in the surprised wooden front door. The incessant telephone never stopped and the restaurant's owners just wanted us back in the kitchen. Beaming radiantly, mother, father and Mort were three just turned on lighthouses. Relieved that I was not flying tonight, I headed for bed.

Without stopping, the doorbell rang over and over again, then the pounding started. Envisioning some crazed benefactor, I ignored it. Picking up the baseball bat, I opened the door and there was the most beautiful girl in the world.

"I couldn't stay away a minute more; you just looked so despondent on the news cast." It was my time and I wasn't going to blow it again. Pulling BJ closer than close, I kissed her with everything that I had, better than anything in the movies I was sure of it. Her dad must have been sure of it to as he stepped out of the shadows and cleared his voice.

"That should do it CJ, not to make more of this than is necessary." But it was necessary; it was love. And love had its way.

"I am not leaving you again; I also want to help the kids in Africa." BJ handed me a box of discarded tennis shoes, really cool ones too, the expensive over the top kind. My girl not only loved me but loved others. The tied-up knot in my stomach loosened itself. Pent-up joy exploded; my heart was given back to me.

THE MELTDOWN

W hen some things mended so easily other things ripped apart. Maybe all the excitement was just too much for dad. During the night he woke up in excruciating pain. Unable to move his arms and legs, dad lay sobbing on his saturated mattress.

During his war stint, Mort had seen it before. After massive trauma, seizure like symptoms invaded the body. It was a neurological nightmare; only heavy narcotics stopped it. Intervention was called.

As if a stomped on fragile vase, mother broke apart. Shrieking, she scurried into the bunkroom locking the door behind her. As Mort cradled dad I tried in vain to get to mother, but the door wouldn't budge. I remembered that mother liked an open window at night so I undid the screen and looked for her but she wasn't anywhere. There was an empty bottle on her bed and then I spotted her slumped over figure on the floor. Yelling intensely, I watched frantically as Mort somehow pried open the door. Instructions were wild birds that flew.

"Get some ice, water, pillows for her head and a blanket. Quickly, move quickly there is no time to lose."

I was close to becoming an orphan and knew it. Panicking, my feet wouldn't budge.

Mort flashed back to his war days. "Soldier, move now, it's an order." I moved. Mort started CPR on mother and I watched even afraid to touch her.

"She's your mother right? Hold her head up. Don't be afraid. Put water on her. Keep propping her neck up. You love her don't you? Act like it. Talk to her about anything, just make it up." With that said, I made it up and told mother the most fantastic things that I never did.

The ambulance attendants burst through the door but were confused.

"Who did we come for?" I lay curled up next to Mother, talked non-stop, and hoped that I would wake up from this personal nightmare.

"The man in the other room and this lady both need assistance," Mort retorted. The attendant realized that Mort was casually direct for the boy's sake so he followed suit.

"Son, let us take care of this. We are trained to do this." As if in a trance, I left the room, grabbed my mitt and went outside. From the opened window, I overheard every word.

"What happened here? Are these relatives of yours? The man in the other room was twisted like a pretzel. I don't know if he can be untwisted. Heavy medication may stop the pain but he needs serious care. This lady was pretty far gone. Hopefully we can pump it all out. The ambulance was oversized so we can take both of them. Are you and the boy all right?"

Mort really didn't want the conversation and made it known. The sooner this ambulance left, the better. He didn't know if CJ or he were ready for the aftermath.

The oak tree wasn't used to the pounding. My ball had smashed it at least a thousand times. The ambulance scurried down the street with its sirens quickening everyone's heart-beat, thankful that they weren't in it. Then I heard his voice.

"Son, everything will be okay. Your parents just needed to be patched up a bit. Within hours, I expect your mother to be back. Our brains are funny instruments. They all handle trauma differently. Sometimes our brains just refuse to handle any of it."

"You mean like mother?"

"Yes, it was just too much for her. Her emotions were a Paraná and devoured her. I don't know which is worse: to feel almost nothing like me or to feel too much like your mother. It's easier my way but I don't know if it is really the best way. She will be calmer with the medicine that they gave her. That's the most important first step in one's therapy, being able to control yourself. The rest just follows into place."

"Mort, you're not going to leave me are you?" My lifeless arms wrapped around Mort before I knew why. And I cried like a baby. My mind was mush and my heart wasn't far behind. Mort held on to me and wouldn't let me go. Our tears crossed one another's faces.

"Not if I have anything to say about it." Mort turned up the radio full blast. Neither one of us wanted to think our own thoughts. As if he were waiting for an eclipse, Mort kept the lights ablaze.

Clanging off the hook, the phone finally told, mother was fixable, out of danger and would be coming home tomorrow. Fully awake, mother demanded to talk to me. Only part of me reached for the phone.

"CJ, I just wanted to hear your voice. I had to hear it. Thank you for saving me. All that I remember were those fantastic stories that you told me. They just never stopped. You really didn't do those things did you?"

"No, mom. My imagination did. Is dad with you?"

"No, they took him to a different unit; this unit is full of stomach aches."

"One down, one to go," offered Mort as he made a Hawaiian concoction of juices and rum and suggested I take a couple of swigs. After drinking half of it, I cratered into nothingness.

Mort would have to wait for the fall by himself. Instinctively, Mort knew the next phone call wasn't going to be so easy. He wished he also was a seventh grader so he wouldn't have to answer it. He didn't think Mr. Sanger was coming home. But CJ's dad was his whole life. He wished his own sons loved him one smidgen as much.

Tomorrow was Sunday; there would be time for what needed to be done. It rang an ominous ring. A frantic voice cried out for CJ. Mort carefully nudged the boy and CJ took the call.

"Son, I'm not coming home any time soon. You take care of your mother and that happy go lucky aide of yours. It's time to find your list, the one we made in the park so long ago. Things will change pretty fast. All that I ask is for you to be ready. CJ, our mitts will always be together out on that baseball field no matter what." And with that said, the phone clicked off.

Everything was very quiet when I awoke. No coffee brewing, no eggs flipped, nothing moved. All that I remembered was that dad talked about a list and our mitts. Looking for that list, I found it stuffed under my book shelf near my violin case. Seeing what I wrote was one thing doing it was quite another. The muffled silence stung me after having so much hope, so much possibility.

When the front door bell rang, fear nagged. It was a very young attendant who escorted mother into the house.

"Good as new probably better than she ever was. Mrs. Sager talked my head off on the way over here. She probably thought I was one of her son's friends."

The young man looked sheepishly at Mort shrugging his shoulders. Was he waiting for a tip? After all he had made a very special delivery. Mort placed a bill in his hand and with that he disappeared.

Mother was calmed, but different. Her eyes were lost, her words far away. Maybe she just wanted some time to recover. She didn't.

"CJ, they fixed me up pretty well. I feel better now. I'm sorry if I caused you to panic, if I caused you any worry at all. It was not my intention. Just seeing your father in such agony unglued me. Will you ever be able to forgive me?"

Everything in me cried out to my mother. Who was I to forgive?

"Mother, we'll be okay. We just have to pick up who we are and what we have left and go forward."

It sounded like a mayor's speech. Mother bought it but I don't know if I really did. Then the strong winds hit. "Dad, what about dad?"

"Since yesterday, I haven't seen your father. The unit where I stayed was for stomach aches. Your dad had much more serious problems."

Right then, I did too. My choice had been made for me: mother, not dad, not the way I planned it. Mort was mother's aide for that one and only day. It was just the beginning of the storm. Tomorrow's deluge washed me away.

THE DELUGE

A s I approached the house, bright yellow tape surrounded me. I couldn't get in fast enough. But a uniformed police officer prevented me from crossing the tape.

"This house is out of bounds for you. Since no one made the mortgage payments, it has been repossessed by the bank."

"But I live here." A tornado of jumbled up clothes was scattered all over the yard. Shirts, jeans, sneakers, all my stuff was basking in the hot sun.

"Not any more kid. If I were you I would grab what you can before anyone else helped themselves. Anything outside the yellow tape was fair game. Some eager beavers already inquired. But I knew these clothes belonged to someone. Your mother packed up her stuff and was given thirty minutes to get it done. Just so that you know, a final notice was sent out but no one replied. Sorry, kid, that it had to go this way. But rules are rules especially with banks. We're just here as back-up making sure everything goes smoothly."

Was this guy for real, is that what he meant? It wasn't going to go smoothly. Screaming my head off, I busted through the yellow tape.

As if in a trance, mother just sat on the bed and stared straight ahead. She looked at me in disbelief.

"I just assumed that your father took care of the house payments. I never knew. I never asked."

So this was the big change that dad mentioned. Dad must have run out of money; his pride wouldn't let him tell. The police officer barged in and demanded that we leave but we didn't move. He too had a son and backed off. The thirty minutes was extended.

The suitcase wasn't packed and lay open on the bed. Where was Mort? He was long gone. Dad's voice echoed in my mind, 'take care of your mother.' Cramming all kinds of things in the suitcase, I tried to comfort her. Jumbled up, mother's mind wandered. Mine needed to be very clear. I felt at least sixteen, old enough to take over and maybe even drive.

"Mother, well just pack our things up, and load up the car." She gave me a strange look, shook her head, and whimpered.

"There was no car. This morning, they came and towed it away. Mort went out to stop them and they arrested him for battery and hauled him away." Anger suffocated me. Taking Mort, our car, our house, we were the battered and homeless. My tears were swarming bees that covered my face. Mother would never see them.

Right before my battered eyes, I became dad.

"Let's just do what we need to do. We will figure the rest out as we go along. Mother, is there anyone that you could call that might put us up for a few days?"

"We have already been marked and branded, the others. No one wants anything to do with us now. We are no longer members of the right club." I wasn't going to argue with her but I would prove her wrong.

Our suitcases were jammed packed but there was nowhere to take them. Then I remembered the club for the others, The YMCA and recently it was converted to include families. It wasn't all that far from here; a good long walk would do us good. Just before we left, the police officer tossed me my baseball mitt.

"Son, I don't think you want to leave this behind. My son never would." Maybe there was some goodness in him after all. Amidst the struggle, I completely forgot about my mitt. But I didn't forget my violin. Thank goodness it had an overhaul strap that fit over my shoulder. So we were off, carried all that we owned, our love for one another and hope that someone would care.

By the time we got to the shelter, we were bedraggled, exhausted and desperate. Immediately we were interviewed, as if they had a job opening, drilled about this and that, and our circumstances.

"Carrying any firearms, knives, sharpened material of any kind? Have you been incarcerated, arrested, or have relatives behind bars?" Sam, the once incarcerated interviewer liked my mother's looks. Putting him in his place, I accidently slammed my violin case on his foot. Our interview ended abruptly and we were given a grand tour of the establishment.

The whole place reeked of chlorine. Everything that came in or out was covered with it, something about germs and prevention. It was worse than any bathroom's odor. The men's quarter was a huge room packed full of bunk beds, one on top of the other with little breathing space.

There was a group shower, just like in gym, more like wash stations with absolute no privacy. Shyness wasn't permitted. The only allowed shower times were early in the morning. Out by eight and back by five was the programmed schedule. Passing the cafeteria, most of the diners were covered with tattoos and mismatched clothes. Mother and I were the best dressed in the place which wasn't to our advantage.

Sam told us that we qualified for a room and led us right around the corner, the family section. The rooms were tiny but each had a door and a small bathroom. The doors didn't look like they really worked; maybe they were just for show. But before I could test one out, we were ushered inside a small room: a single bed with a folding chair and tiny table. I was one of the three bears in Goldie Locks. Could this all be a fairy tale? If it were, I wanted more than anything to wake up. I pinched myself but the bedroom didn't disappear.

"Dinner was served until seven o'clock. Get there early or you won't get any. First come first served."

With that said, Sam walked away looking like he wanted me to vanish. But I wasn't going anywhere. Laughing hysterically, we closed the door and collapsed.

"If my friends at school could see me now, they would think it was so cool." My words melted in the room's heat and our laughter faded into tears. Mother looked as if she would jump out of her skin. Without permission, our creature comforts were ripped away from us. That old adage,' You don't know what you have until you lose it,' fit just perfectly.

The cafeteria's food wasn't worth all of the hassle. Before we went to the cafeteria, mother removed all of her makeup and changed into one of my dad's shirts that I packed. Being hit on by Sam. an ex-con was not to her liking. Once in line we were ignored until a burly man just went through us, pushing us out of the way. No rules applied. You got in line, tried to stay in it, and got your food or didn't. It was all purely chance.

"Enjoy your food, and eat as fast as you can," offered the cafeteria attendant. The lumpy potato concoction filled me. Since it wasn't her diet food, Mother mouthed and barely finished it. Her strawberry Ozarka bottled water wasn't waiting for her in her room.

There would be no bus in the morning so I needed to get up an hour earlier and walk to school. The water barely came out of the showerhead and the toilet barley flushed.

Mother was asleep hoping to wake up from the surreal surroundings. It gave me time to think about bashed-in Mort.

Lying close to the cement floor, Mort probably stared behind bars listening to men scream and jeer. Choking on chlorine, Mort's cell surely reeked of it.

Dad suffered more than any of us, all twisted up, alone, and without anyone to love. Before I left I could almost hear what mother would go through today.

When Victoria awoke from her restless sleep, her son was long gone. According to the non- negotiable rules taped to the battered door, she missed breakfast and had 20 minutes to vacate. Makeup which once defined her was no longer a part of her daily routine. Should she even bother brushing her hair?

Then Victoria remembered today was the day to get some kind of a job. Anything would do just to keep her busy until CJ returned from school. With just a little lipstick, Victoria's tired face lit up. This was temporary she told herself, over in just a few weeks. There had to be an answer somewhere and she would find it. A retest, that was what it was; since she failed the first test when her husband crumpled up like a pretzel. Her mind wouldn't allow her to go back. But CJ had nothing to do with any of this; why did her son have to suffer?

Once on the street, Victoria realized that the only thing that she really knew how to do was cook. Her old life revolved around shopping, gossiping, and visiting with her friends. No one had the slightest idea that she could prepare food. When she was younger, her mother made her fix two, nutritious, filling, and balanced meals a week for her family. Instead of enjoying the task, she loathed it and vowed never to cook again.

A dangling sign almost clonked her in the face. 'Sous chef wanted, inquire within.' The restaurant didn't look like much from the outside but neither did she.

"Chop these vegetables, combine this pork and create a dressing." Victoria was back in high school as her mother hovered over her shoulder. She understood little of the broken English minced with Chinese but the food spoke to her.

The job was hers and she started tomorrow. Wong, her new boss fixed her a plate of shredded sirloin mixed with greens and heaped up a bowl of Wong Tong Soup. For breakfast? She stared. Starving, she inhaled it.

Oddly quiet and still, the decorated room hid her as she blended in with the shadows and Chinese tapestries. Her fellow- workers were shorter and tinier. Gleeful and unhurried, they bobbed and walked. Every step was in harmony, full of purpose. Peacefulness saturated her. If they could make it; she would follow in their bobbing footsteps. Their language was a sing-song, musical ups and downs. She preferred it to her own language. Maybe she could learn it. Hope rose up in her like steamed percolated coffee but was quickly snuffed out.

In no hurry, Victoria absorbed the sidewalk sights as she walked back. A car pulled over and called out her name.

"Oh I'm so sorry, I thought I knew you. The way you walked just reminded me of her. Victoria remembered that she had worn a cap so that her hair wasn't noticed. Margaret's next words bit into her like a frigid piece of Alaskan ice. "Can I help you out? Would twenty dollars do?" Victoria wanted to scream, to cry out, to plead, but nothing came out of her. Pride silenced her. Margaret practically flung twenty dollars out the car's window and pulled away abruptly without glancing back.

Victoria's spirit moaned. Her best friend didn't know her. Was makeup that deceiving? The door of friendship and acceptance slammed shut in Victoria's face. The rejection stung. Life as she once knew it retreated. There was no going back.

Meanwhile at school CJ thought that he was ready for his peers, but he wasn't. His usual gooey stilted hairstyle was a miss, his shirt was more than wrinkled, and his swagger evaporated into thin air. He even smelled different. His cool cologne was long forgotten in his repossessed house.

The love of his life was supposed to be back in school but BJ was nowhere in sight. Did the whole school already know the shocking secret? Unprepared for his classes, CJ felt his teachers peer right through him. Forgetting his violin, he skipped practice. Overnight, his inner music changed. He couldn't hear a single sound. CJ wore a visible sign, damaged goods. The cool kids wouldn't even come near him. As he walked by, Markus, his baseball team's first baseman, stuffed a newspaper under his arm.

"Did you know that you're famous, but not in a good way? It's all about you on the second page." Leprosy struck. There was a picture of our house, what was left of it with a question mark and commentary, 'What happens when you least expect it?' Panicking, my thirteen-year old breath got stuck in my chest. The secret was out. Even Chad, my former fellow chef on African night, passed by and didn't even look at me. The death knoll chimed. Looking for my real friends, I never found any. At the end of the day, I was summoned to the counselor's office.

"CJ, your status has changed. You're no longer listed here in the district. We need proof of your homestead." I explained that we were looking for a house but it might take some time. The counselor informed me that there was a three-week grace period with very few exceptions. School left a very bad taste in my mouth and I didn't know which was worse, being homeless or being a needy exception.

WITHOUT

Anxious days scurried by without a breath or word from dad. Knowing nothing wasn't acceptable. Wanting the past to stay in the past, Mother never talked about dad. Every day, Mother looked more and more Chinese. Her waking thoughts focused on how to prepare Chinese greens and combine shredded meats.

It would take someone of keen smarts to find dad. Mort busted through. But where would I find Mort? One holding pen or cell was as good as another.

Visiting the local jails was out of my comfort zone. Only thirteen, I needed a tougher look so I smeared bits of smudged charcoal on my face that gave me that close forgotten shaved shadow. Funny, how the more I lounged for facial hair, only the hair on my head grew faster. I also tore a few permanent holes in my jeans and wore a baggy shirt.

Mort was a long lost uncle who needed to be found. Standing in no man's land in front of the jailer, my words jumbled up. No one fit Mort's description so the officer told me to go check the local probationary unit. Luck followed me. During the middle of leisure time, I spied Mort over in the corner playing cards with an empty chair.

"Mort, it's CJ. He turned around but I didn't recognize him. Battered and bruised, his face was a swollen watermelon. "Your face what happened to your face?"

"When I jumped on the uniformed lookout back at your house, two other determined officers piled on top of me. Punching practice, rage got the best of me. Your mom just couldn't grasp that all her stuff was taken from her. Living on the streets was no big deal for me, but for the two of you it was ridiculous."

"Thank you for your rage and your good intentions. By chance, we found a temporary shelter." I wanted to tell Mort that sometimes I went to all of my classes and sometimes I didn't. And without dad, everything blurred. And that mother turned Chinese. But I didn't. My insides burned but a man never showed it. "Will you help me find dad?"

"You know son you might not be prepared for what you find. He may not, well let's face that when we find him. Good behavior will probably get me out of here soon enough, another few days at the most. My bruises have turned into a plumish purple, quite the fashion statement. Even in here, it turned a few heads The lightweights are all scared of me. Getting back to your dad, have you checked any of the treatment centers? It would probably be a long-term care facility. But seeing what happened, I don't know if your dad had any money at all for emergencies. What I am trying to say is that he might be in a place of last resort, where the poorest go. CJ do you really want to find your dad knowing that he will not be anything like you remembered him?"

"Yes," it was the only word that made any sense.

"Oh another thing, there's something waiting for you at the police station. You'll have to go down and get it. The lookout wanted it for his son but he told me that he would hold it for you for a short time. About your living arrangements, make sure that you lock your door wherever you are staying. And don't trust anyone with anything."

"We are staying at the YMCA and the lock on the door doesn't work. Creepy men covered with tattoos are everywhere. I was surprised that they let us in without one."

"You also need to let your mother know that at any time your room is up for grabs. They never let you know; just be ready to leave. CJ you will have to develop some street sense. More than likely that's where you'll end up."

"But I'm just a kid."

"That doesn't matter now." Saying good bye to Mort made me feel much better. Nothing that he said cheered me up. I would find dad without his help.

The police station was right around the block. When the officer remembered me, I wished that he hadn't. Their uniforms were misleading. They went by the book with everything they said, but who knew if they meant any of it. I signed a paper and then the officer told me to go back to the old shed which was behind the station. A bit scuffed up like me, there was my bike. What was a kid without his wheels? Getting mine back, my legs were grateful that something else could carry me. But where would I keep it? This shed would do for now. It was only a block away from the shelter. Suddenly finding dad got a lot easier.

Once on my bike, my swagger returned. Vicki, the angelic flirting nurse back on my dad's forgotten hospital ward dashed into my mind. It was more than a thought. She would know where to look.

Vicki was visibly disturbed with the news of dad's recent trauma but jotted down a list of possible places where he might be. When we sat down at an extra long table in the nurse's station, her fluttering wings paused.

"CJ, do you think that there's some reason why your dad hasn't contacted you?"

"Sure, he has no idea where we are."

"Do you know that the mind is a very sensitive instrument and anything can set it off?"

"Sure, I guess that's why school no longer interests me. My mind is an over- stuffed closet and I can't shut the door." Vicki peered at me with those same eyes that I remembered, kindness, compassion, mixed with sadness, lounging to help but had professional boundaries. "Vicki, don't worry, I just needed some names. Did you know a boy and his bike can do almost anything?" Vicki grabbed and hugged me as her stammering tears dripped, so much for professional boundaries.

Most of the places were beyond the hospital and Vicki penned the addresses on a scribbled map that she quickly made. The first couple of places I peered into, fancy furniture, golden picture frames and chandeliers stared back at me. Dad wouldn't be there; I moved on. But there it was right in front of me, as if to say don't even bother. It was an elderly home whose rusty peeling painted sign dangled in the wind. "The End of the Road Ministries' said it all. Old vines hung over the roof's awnings. Some of the windows were cracked, even broken. How could anything so neglected take care of others? I didn't care what the sign said; I knew that everything that meant anything was in this place.

As I walked slowly down the dreary, narrow halls, no one even noticed me. A few nurses scurried here and there, dawning white caps and furrowed frowns. Nobody even smiled until I bumped into him. He was a curiously tall man who looked like he was in charge.

"Son, are you sure you are in the right place? There are no children here. Our patients never leave. They have no visitors. They are the forgotten. But you haven't forgotten. Who are you looking for?" I couldn't stand it any longer. My knees bent and I collapsed. The curious man gently picked me up and set me carefully down in a cushy chair that was in the hallway. An elderly lady walked slowly by and patted my head and called me her Marky. Stopping abruptly, she wanted to know why I was so skinny. Her eyes danced like a child and she murmured and chatted to herself quite contentedly. At first she scared me, but then I realized she just needed someone to listen. But her attention span didn't last long and she scurried down the hall out of sight.

The curious man, Mr. Rootin, came back with a cold Coca cola and a few oatmeal raisin cookies.

"I always liked these when I was a kid. I guess that I still do and try to keep a few on hand for guests. Who was it that you haven't forgotten?"

"It's my dad; he got all crunched up; we couldn't straighten him out. An ambulance took him away and that was the last time I saw him. Without my dad I'm nothing." Mr. Rootin laid his hand on my shoulder and paused. "Well let's see if we can find your dad."

Each room was covered with faded wall paper and what you touched was old, and discarded. Two or three patients were crammed together chatting away to themselves and most didn't notice us. Bed bound, some of the hands colored and fit puzzles together. None of it made much sense to me. These people were much too old for coloring. I was even too old for coloring.

"Anything to keep them busy; they don't remember much from one minute to the next."

"Are they all that way?"

"Yes, that's why it was called the end of the road. These minds will never work again." My stomach knotted up as we came into a smaller room with one bed. The patient, curled up in a ball, didn't even seem to breathe. When his eyes met mine, tears exploded down his hollow cheeks. Blocked words. With my arms around him, I rocked him slowly back and forth. A scared animal that wanted out, he started shrieking and Mr. Rootin gave him a shot to calm him down. But there was no way out. I pulled dad into myself knowing that I would never see him again. Time had run away from both of us. Before I left, I tucked my heart inside Dad's hands and ran as fast as I could and never looked back. I didn't stop to breathe.

Cutting through the fields, I hit a huge rock and went over my bike's handle bars. Maybe if I smashed myself up. I would get put next to dad. Blood trickled down my face and hurt covered me. A deep saturating pain pounded in my chest where my heart used to be. It was too much. I cried for dad, for me, for our lives that were so randomly taken from us. I even cried for mom who didn't know and would never know. A deep sleep overcame me.

When I awoke it was dark, way too dark. The shelter's curfew was eight o'clock. You made it or you didn't. There were no ifs or buts. At the shelter's battered door, the ink-stamped ex-con informed me that our room was needed. An abused mother with three little kids needed a refuge. Supposedly, mother left a few hours ago. She wouldn't just leave me; would she? In the very back of the shelter underneath a tall spreading oak tree, I saw brush pulled over my violin, mitt, and two unsuspecting suitcases. Through the overgrown grasses, I spied mother. I couldn't get to her fast enough and broke apart in her arms.

"You found him didn't you? I just couldn't tell you. It was better for you never to know. Now, truly alone, there will never be any going back for anything or anyone. It will be what we make of it." My arms refused to let her go. "There's a Chinese lantern waiting for us in the restaurant's loft. We will be safe there."

"There was no such thing as safe." Little did I know how true my words were.

THE LOFT

Creaky, dusty stairs led up to the Chinese loft. Big squishy, red pillows were piled high on the floor. It was a place for refugees. I was grateful to Mr. Wong who insisted that we stay. Around us were the needy, the homeless. I was a giant, twice the size of the other boys. The air was filled with sing-song jabbering. A small decorated tray of fortune cookies and warm pots of tea welcomed us. I couldn't remember a time when I had so little but felt so much. Not understanding a word around me, I felt warmth and acceptance. Darting eyes and smiles washed through my broken soul. They knew something that I didn't. I was determined to find out where it was. Then and there, I decided not to go back to school. I no longer had to prove anything to anyone. There was no longer anyone to please. Just surviving took everything out of me. The desire to become anything else vanished.

"Don't wake me up early tomorrow. My ears can't listen anymore, my eyes can't see." Mother pulled me closer. "CJ, a little time away from school won't hurt anything." My burden lifted. Wafting in soothing almond incense, my mind relaxed as I succumbed to sleep.

Early in the morning, chanting and singing echoed around me. Squatted figures perched and waited. From out of the shadows, Mr. Wong appeared. He took his rightful place in the middle of the circle and jabbered Chinese. The others sang in a muffled chorus, a symphony of sounds. Clean, crisp white uniform smocks were passed out. Mr. Wong stood by my side and looked beyond me dropping one of the freshly laundered smocks in my lap. No one needed to tell me that Kitchen duty was in my horizon. I mean after all, I was a weekend chef. One by one, we got ready for the day. Around the corner, private showers waited for us. Cleanliness was a must and privacy was guaranteed.

Mother stirred quickly knowing that there was much preparation to do. Instinctively, I was by her side. Distinct, our whitish chief hats couldn't be missed. The two of us chopped vegetables, greens, spices, and meats which had to be ready when the demanding customers arrived.

The busy bustle of our school's cafeteria was nothing compared to this. Before ten o'clock, hungry customers lined up outside and waited impatiently for a table. This must be the place for lunch as menus were hurriedly handed out and orders taken.

In an excitable voice, Mr. Wong quickly pulled off my hat and handed me an order pad, "Menu number on paper." With that said I was thrown into a sea of bobbing heads and shrill voices. Much to my surprise many spoke to me in English.

Hands full of various combined foods, Mother worked tirelessly, as overflowing plates ran out of the kitchen. Never even seeing mother lift a plate, my mouth fell open.

"CJ close your mouth; it is very unbecoming." A pride filled balloon rose inside me. Mother changed; she no longer depended on anyone else to make her way. It was the very first time that I was proud to be her son. Her friends were obsolete, her makeup, if any, was smudged, her hands were raw and blistered but there was that glow, wisdom's survival. The smile that burst from her face confirmed it.

"CJ, if your dad took care of us, so can I." Mr. Wong bustled about greeting all of his guests with over-sized fortune cookies. Mr. Wong personally chose the fortunes wanting to spread good will to each and every one. Some of that goodness must have rubbed off on me.

After the lunch rush, footsteps were softer and heads relaxed. Sitting together, small hands quickly passed numerous bowls full of sauces, some dark some light that challenged your taste buds. Over flowing bowls of white and fried rice accompanied them. Fairly skillful with chop sticks, I blended right in with the others. No one said a word but concentrated on the food.

It was nothing like school. My friends didn't care if they ate or not. Well fed, they had no idea what it was like to go without. Did I even have any so called friends? Surely they would have looked for me. Maybe they were glad that the catcher's position on the baseball team was finally up for grabs. Maybe they were glad the spot next to BJ was available. And what about BJ, my best friend that I thought was forever? There was no forever; never again would I allow myself to give that much to a girl.

A little hand grabbed mine and led me outside where overstuffed gold fish swam unhindered in a very small pond. In class, I remembered reading that water was very important to the Chinese. There were tiers in the pond that were supposed to be levels of excellence. The water represented life and what they were supposed to achieve. The Chinese were one huge baseball team, everything was a group effort focused on team work. I was too much of a loner, a self achiever, to ever fit into that way of thinking.

The little Chinese girl gazed at me with wondering eyes. Grinning, her fingers slanted my eyes. She hummed a small tune and stopped. Big water drops dripped down her cheeks. I couldn't believe that I made a little girl cry. Around girls, I was worthless.

"CJ, that's Yang Moon who just lost her brother, offered Mr. Wong. He got himself into something that wouldn't let him go. It devoured him. My intervention was too late and not enough. They literally dragged him away and that was the last time anyone saw him. He was a few years older than you and thought he knew everything. Greed got the best of him. He just couldn't say no to a flashy car and flashy friends. There was no truth. The money pulled him under." Mr. Wong's wisdom spoke. Money meant nothing to me. It was just there, or used to be. But something was missing that he didn't say. It would have to wait. Yang Moon yearned to see her brother again. My yearning was gone.

As days passed, I noticed things, things that I overlooked. Some of the kids knew English but never talked to me. Talking amongst themselves, they always watched to see what I did.

"We don't belong here," readily announced Sung, a young teenage boy. Confused, I was the one who didn't belong. "We hide and work, always afraid, always careful." What did he mean?

"What exactly are you afraid of?"

"The men take us away. Maybe we go without saying goodbye." Our conversation was unfinished. Mr. Wong interrupted us. "Idle lips sink ships." It was an unwrapped Chinese fortune that wouldn't appear in any cookie.

Mother was too tired to notice anything. That night, Kids huddled closer to their parents. Candles were unlit. Since there was some kind of a meeting in the restaurant, Mr. Wong insisted on quiet, the calm before the storm.

Unannounced, demanding voices burst through the front door and deafened the air.

"Where are they? We know they're here So many waiters at lunch were a dead give a way." Around me, whole families vanished. It wasn't a drill and hiding spots were well defined. Mother and I were at a loss and didn't move a muscle. "There's two of them over there. Nope, not what we came for."

"What are you looking for?" I boldly asked the hurried man who almost tripped over me.

"You don't need to know kid; it doesn't concern you. Let's get out of here. There's too many eyes and ears tonight." The three men disappeared as quickly as they came.

Bellowing from below wafted up the stairs. "Nobody was grabbed; they're gone. Somebody forgot to lock the door. Tomorrow, there will be a new lock." Who was Mr. Wong kidding? A new lock wouldn't stop these guys. They were blood hounds that already knew the scent. The comfort and warmth that once saturated me vanished. That nagging thought washed through me again, there was no safe.

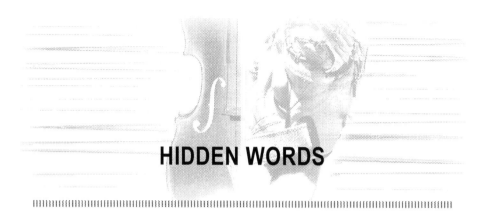

HIDDEN WORDS

A s if a forgotten nightmare, nobody even mentioned the intruders. It was chores as usual, but I was not one to give up so easily. Just as predicted, some of the fatherless, the threes left without a goodbye. With less help, the work load was more demanding. No longer in training, I welcomed the challenge.

Promoted to head chef, mother tucked me under her arm. As her assistant, whatever I said ears listened.

Mr. Wong pulled me aside. "CJ, you need to learn some Chinese phrases to encourage and lead the others. I will teach you. When I'm not here, you will be the man in charge." So in between lunches our lessons began. There was an un-easiness between us; I poked at it.

"If you want me to lead, shouldn't I know what I am up against?"

"You have already seen it. Last night they were peaceful, often that is not the case. The workers are here at their own risk. I can only go so far to protect them."

"What about us?"

"You are a different people; not one of ours." Your eyes don't see what we see and your ears don't hear what we hear. You will both be safe as long as you know little." In history, I remembered reading about the slaves and how their masters cared and feed them, but still punished and refused to allow them to read and write. Without knowledge individuals were nothing but prey. My fellow workers and I were not going to be prey to anyone. How ignorant I was.

It was the night of the big celebration. One hundred people or more were supposed to attend. Huge trays of shell fish, lean meat, slippery buttery noodles and sautéed vegetables pranced out of the kitchen. Plum wine was a running facet. Mr. Wong insisted that our uniformed white jackets were pressed and starched; they were tighter and more constricting. Somebody dropped a tray and then all pandemonium broke loose. Insults were geese that flew swiftly across the room. Anger saturated anything that moved. Fists flew and heads ducked. Then I saw what I had only seen in the movies. The light caught the blade and danger flashed. Women shrieked, waiters ran. Another metal flashed, Mr. Wong was hand cuffed and carried towards the door like a sack of potatoes. This time nobody was safe. Undercover federal agents swarmed the premises. It was a torn apart beehive. Yang Moon's brother wasn't the only knee deep in corruption. Evidently, Mr. Wong taught him everything he knew.

The words drugs, illegals spewed out of their mouths. What I saw was equal to any spy thriller. Turning around a few times, I convinced myself that it was real, much too real.

"Boy, you remind me of my son and need to get out of here before you are taken in with the others." Everything in me said listen, but I didn't. A locomotive of pent-up rage surged through me. My Chinese friends shouldn't be punished for working and trying to feed themselves. Mr. Wong's gun was hidden in the loft. I couldn't get to it fast enough. Before I knew it, the gun spewed fireworks that seemingly went off by itself. It was enough. Legs scrambled and arms tore. Lights were shot out; darkness enveloped the deception.

"Wong, he got away, he's gone. Let's get out of here. Without him we don't stand a chance." Somehow mother found her way to the loft's stairs and pulled the gun out of my hand.

"It's not time to die; it's time to leave." It sounded like something from Shakespeare. Mother's face was ashen and she looked like a scared gorilla from the zoo, ready to protect at any cost. "You have done enough; now you will follow me." Mother in her innate wisdom had also pried and questioned. Tunnels, there were undisclosed tunnels that led out to the woods behind the restaurant.

If we were to survive, we had to get out of the commotion. Deep into the woods we ran, stumbled, and fell. Mother couldn't go any further. Her adrenalin rush ended as quickly as it began. Up ahead, there was a tattered shed that offered shelter. Tall sticky grasses whipped our legs and tree branches taunted us, pulled us back, and threw us down. Mother and I propped each other up as we stumbled into the broken-up doorway. The door was half gone. We blended in nicely. Filled water jugs were piled up in a corner. Three cans of beans were in the nearly empty cupboard right beside a jar of mostly gone coffee. A broken fishing pole leaned against the back of the wall. An old pot- bellied stove just waited for any kind of wood. Nestled under some old towels a dwindling pile of firewood caught my eye. Mother shivered. Somewhere, there had to be matches. An old rusty jar held the answer. Before long, a starter fire shone back at us.

The lazy flames licked away at time. I was once again with my dad camping out in the woods. He wanted to make sure that if I ever got lost, I could survive. We started a fire with sticks, a stone, and a small piece of glass. All that I heard was 'If you were in control, everything around you knew it.' But I wasn't in control and everything knew it. There was an old mattress piled under some debris in the corner. Mother was asleep. I stuffed forgotten rags in the cracked opening in the door. If anything ripped the door apart, I would hear it. Allowing myself to slip away into uncertainty, everything faded.

Before the sun rose, I rose. In no time at all, two steaming cups of coffee waited for us. The word homeless took another dimension. It was time to leave for nowhere. There had to be other shelters, other restaurants, other . . . It was time for the talk.

As if back home, Mother was up and busied herself.

"CJ, this coffee, it's better than mine."

"Mother,"

CJ, please call me Victoria. It just sounds easier, has a simpler ring to it, a needed change."

"That's it; that's exactly right. Victoria you don't need me. You can do better without me. A woman alone has a better chance to make it. I'm just extra baggage." Much to my horror, there was no reply. I didn't really mean any of it but it sounded so right.

"Listen carefully to what I have to say. We will make it together or not at all." I heard love, saw love, felt love for the very first time from Victoria. She really wanted me to be with her. The talk ended abruptly, never to be brought up again.

"Since we're traveling light, we need to get moving. No telling when that fisherman will come back for his pole and beans." A broad smile danced across Victoria's face and mine. Hope in one another was all that we had. It was enough.

THE TRACKS

W ay in the back of my mind, I remembered how Dad talked about the train, the beauty of seeing everything pass you by so effortlessly. But the beauty wasn't buckled in a train car with other passengers; it was stowed away in the empty cars. As a young boy he couldn't afford the passage and it was the only way for him to see what he only heard about. When he was four, his father died and his mother lost tract of everyone including him. Needing to help out at home, at twelve dad already had a job. The train set him free.

Victoria glanced sideways at me. We headed for the tracks. I mean even if we were caught it wasn't as if it mattered. We didn't have a job to be fired from, or a home to be evicted from, or friends to shun us. What mattered was boarding the train car successfully. It took some kind of skill or others would attempt it. We both had agile, long, skinny legs that were just itching for a challenge. The train cars were covered with graffiti, colorful signs and letters that were in a different language. They were supposed to mean something, some kind of hidden code.

The train slowed. An empty car passed us by Victoria and I challenged the obstacle course, getting up and over and inside the car. With my violin strapped to my back, my hands and legs were free and fell right into place. Tangled up, Victoria wasn't as lucky. One of her legs twisted and nearly missed the mark. From out of nowhere, two strong tanned marked arms reached out and hoisted her up. Grateful, we hung on to one another and collapsed. There was no time for pain, relief took over. Victoria's life no longer revolved around herself.

The marked arms made us as comfortable as possible. Sharing a tin of water and some strewn balled hay, the man motioned for us to rest. He was up to something and everything in me went on red alert. His eyes never left Victoria's face and my eyes never left his. Being around Mr. Wong taught me a thing or two. I was no longer a scared teenager but a man in the making. Hauling those heavy trays around toned up newly formed muscles. My arm muscles flexed and glistened in the light; I made sure that the marked stranger looked.

"Kid, you need to relax. We're all here for a reason. Why don't we just enjoy it and make the most of it? Full of deadness, his eyes were creepy and a horrible rancid odor spewed out of his mouth as he spoke. I almost got sick.

"You don't know anything. We have nothing in common with you. This was just a new way to ride the train."

"Big shot are you kid? Hasn't anyone ever taught you any manners? Is that the way you talk to your elders?"

Victoria slowly uncovered a kitchen knife from her pocket. The marked arms were crab claws that quickly retracted. "Like the kid said, we have nothing in common with one another." Victoria, well mom pumped me full of wonder. Where did that come from?

"Ah lady, I didn't mean anything by it. Just wanted to be friendly that's all." And with that said the decorated arms slid way back into the car out of sight.

We had no idea where the train was headed. The landscape changed, the flatness vanished like our past lives. Small hills and jutted rocks sprung out of nowhere. The rick red, copper color of the ground turned into a golden-brown and taller leafy trees sported heavier branches. New Mexico faded behind us without so much as a good by. Faces of school buddies called out to me. BJ. There was no more time to tell her what needed to be said. Those unspoken words remained forever frozen in my heart.

From out of one of the darkened corners a deeper voice cleared its throat.

"Hope you're ready for a longer ride. This train is on its way to the East Coast, someone said maybe as far as New York. It makes stops along the way so you can get out and grab a bite to eat if you're lucky enough to find others' leftovers."

"He means, kid hit the trash cans and hope it's still wrapped. Sometimes they feel sorry for you and give you a buck or two. The two of you shouldn't have any trouble. you aren't marked yet."

"Ah leave them alone. They'll figure it out as they go along. They shut you up pretty well didn't they?" I wondered what that mark was but swore to myself then and there that Victoria and I would never claim it.

My eyes absorbed everything: pine trees, the green earth, the swooping birds, and the bigness of it all. Exactly what dad said, there were no rules out here, no one told you what you could or couldn't do. It wasn't that I hadn't traveled because I had. With our claim to fame baseball team, we went on a few trips to nearby towns to declare total victory but it was all scheduled and exact. A station-wagon packed full of kids and coaches left nothing to the imagination. Now, our imagination was the only thing that allowed us to survive.

The train's rocking lulled the way over-grown to sleep. Even as Victoria slept she never let go of that knife. The conductor's voice yanked us out of our sleep, something about New Orleans. People scurried this way and that. I was a misplaced bald eagle that watched from a hidden perch. It was time to hunt for food. A can of beans didn't go far.

Instinctively I lowered myself out of the train car and headed for food. The lingering smell of hotdogs and sauerkraut filled my senses and my nose lead me. The take- out stand was just down the street. Mr. Wong's voice rang out in my head, 'save the money that you earned.' Back then, there was nothing else to do with it. Right now, it would keep us alive. Stuffing two hot dogs into my mouth before I even paid for them, I bought four more. The red-faced man who grilled the hotdogs didn't seem at all surprised and waited patiently for me to finish.

"The food isn't going anywhere. Take your time. Not in school today?"

"No, my mother and I decided to take a much-needed vacation. Kind of on the run you might say."

"I understand completely. Just try to keep some kind of balance. That's all that you need to do. Just keep talking to your dad." The red-faced man wouldn't take my money and wrapped up six more hot dogs.

"My dad doesn't talk, doesn't move, and doesn't even know me. And like a gush of sudden torrential rain a storm blew across my face. It was just that this man, this total stranger seemed to care. Why should he? As if on fire, words jumped out of my mouth; the whole shameful mess revealed itself. Then in the distance, I heard the train whistle. I was a good block away. Suddenly food took a back seat.

The empty, lounging golf cart beside the hot dog stand perked up its ears. "Jump in son. I will get you to your train." And he did but not before he stuffed a few bills in my pocket and bid me farewell. With a warm food bag cradled in my arms and a confessed heart, I clamored towards the waiting train car. Victoria was just about to jump off when I appeared out of nowhere.

Now, the inside of the car smelled like a grandmother's kitchen even though I never had one. Once, one of my friends told me that only good things come out of their kitchens, something about love. Usually nothing ever came out of our kitchen except excuses. More than enough, the donated Spartan picnic quickly disappeared. Instinctively, sharing was something the needy learned to do. Others also needed to survive. Food had a way of softening emotions. Hunger drove anyone nuts. And everything was calmed as the train marched down the tracks for its next destination.

Like you could reach up and grab them, the stars never looked closer or brighter as they did that night. In science class, we memorized the constellations. Knowing what to look for, I impressed Victoria and the others. All attention was focused on me. Who knew that I would actually use something that I learned in school. From the naming of the ancients, the history of the constellations gushed out of my mouth: I hadn't impressed anyone since I left school. A promise to myself, I would return to school no matter what. This was no life for a kid, for anyone. I refused to be like any of these older men. Remembering what I told the concerned street vendor that this was just an extended vacation from life until Victoria and I figured things out.

Sleep had its way as it sometimes did. There were no stars when I awoke only the softness of the rising sun. A kaleidoscope of colors brushed the sky. So welcome, the quiet was overpowering. From within me, a still voice rose higher and higher. Our lives had to change. But change and hope grabbed hands. From now on this was our adventure not our condemnation.

During the night, one of the riders jumped out. But nothing altered the steady rhythm of the train With a will of its own, it wasn't bothered with who did or didn't stay on. Determined to be more like that train, I vowed to surge ahead no matter what went on around me. From within the shadows, the sulking stranger pushed and shoved me down behind some hay. Still asleep, Victoria was still covered with the warm straw.

"I heard some voices back here somewhere. Wait until I get my hands on them. Compared to a rotting jail cell, this is luxury. Free loaders, I can smell them. Before we reach the Carolinas, I will find them. A rotting jail cell is just what they need." The voices faded.

A large hand fell on my back. "You need to cover your tracks better. Become street wise if you and your mother plan to survive. Out here, no one will give you a break. Make your own breaks or suffer the consequences. I really hope that you make it kid." The gruffness vanished and a bear of a man quieted. Victoria stirred.

"CJ, why are you all scrunched up? Sleep as comfortably as you can."

"No, sleep as safely as you can." Overhearing bits of the conversation, Victoria realized that jail was indeed a consequence. Victoria was tired of leading and wanted someone, anyone to follow. Weeks ago, her limitations were reached. She would follow her son even to jail. Victoria's hope was a November sunset that dwindled away.

NO AIR

Chugging along, the train steered towards the coast. The smell of heavy salted air and pungent seaweed filled our unaccustomed lungs. The conductor went up and down the rows reminding everyone of the three-hour layover. We couldn't help but overhear. The roar of the ocean pulled us in. There wasn't much water in New Mexico. To me the beach could have been on the other side of the world but now it was right here. Good thing for the shorts in my bag. Swimming in jeans wouldn't work. Beige high-lighted sand dunes slopped besides the churning ocean. Victoria waded in knee deep water. I threw myself into the innocent, deceiving waves. One minute I was upright the next I was a rag doll thrashed about not knowing when or where my feet would land. The waves pulled me under and carried me out away from the shore. Victoria's frantic waving disappeared from sight.

For the very first time in my life I was at the mercy of something that I didn't know, didn't understand. One of my friends once told me that the more you thrashed the more you crashed. Just let the waves carry you out and then eventually you floated back towards shore only if the sharks didn't pull you apart first. The water dragged and spit me out. My eyes, ears, and nose were flooded. My legs didn't work. Then father's voice rang clearly in my ears, 'Son, take care of your mother.' Fits of determination rose up. I was not going to be a lifeless victim in tomorrow's newspaper. We wouldn't miss that train. Little by little I kicked my way in to shore and fell head long on the beach. Completely deserted, there was no one to congratulate me. I must have passed out. When I came to, Victoria was there with shaking tears, and a bottle of water. Dousing my head with cold water brought me to. A beat up trailer pulled over to help.

"You can't trust this water," Marco, a bearded long-haired man proclaimed. "No one swims in it. You are lucky to be alive. Look over there; see the fin? You got out in the nick of time." Three men, each with a beard longer than the other peered at us. Bathing wasn't part of their lifestyle. But then I remembered that saying, 'Calling the kettle black'; we were equally as un-kept.

My teeth chattered relentlessly having their own conversation. Warm, thick blankets were pulled out of the broken-down trailer. Victoria wrapped me in a woolen cocoon as the men built a needed fire started with dried up kelp. Ice chests stuffed with fish appeared out of nowhere: flat, round, brown, speckled and grey, the fish peered out at us. Ready knives cut quickly through the scaled skins leaving glistening white meat. Sharpened arrow like sticks pierced through the headless fish. Buried in the coals the aroma filled the chilled air. Pete, an outgoing member of the shaggy group was on his own fishing expedition.

"You're really out here by yourselves? Victoria muttered something. I spoke up.

"Not really, dad's waiting for us just not here."

"So you are related?" There was no need for this chit-chat. "We got separated on the train that's all."

"Sounds good son, but I don't believe a word of it. No man would leave his family behind."

"Well Pete you left yours behind didn't you?"

"That was different. No matter what, a family should stay together. Now, I know that. You are welcome to share our food and our company for the night. Tomorrow if you like maybe we can catch that train." Pete relaxed his grip on his stoking stick. The ready blackened fish turned everything around. Starving we could hardly wait for our share. The charred meat fell off the bone easily and numerous fish were consumed. Sam one of the silent runners brought back a jug of clear wine from out of the rig. It was passed around the circle of contented eyes. The fire's warmth warmed our minds as well as our bodies. Sam pulled out a guitar and songs effortlessly sprung out of us. It was a scene from a Boy scouts' extravaganza: a beach, a smoldering fire, blackened fish, and a melodic guitar. For one night, we were happy to be part of the troop. Giddy, one by one the men retired for the evening. Some kind of smelly smoke seeped out of cracks in the trailer. Victoria and I were thankful we weren't in it. Nothing moved us away from this fire. Appearances deceived. Men who looked so menacing turned out to be so harmless. Once the lit kerosene lamps went out, there was no movement of any kind.

A shooting star exploded in the night sky, known to be a sign, a change, something good. Deep down I knew that if the heavens were in such ordered balance our steps were equally protected. Warmth saturated me as the waves lulled us to sleep. Pulled out of a deep sleep, something bit me right in the toe. Its big brown eyes rolled around on stalks. It was more of a love bite and I challenged it to a duel. With claws raised, I couldn't help but wonder at its courage since I was a thousand times bigger even lying on the sand. My laughing frightened it away.

Morning rose in a burning red orange marmalade sky. The smell of bacon drifted towards us. These men sure knew how to eat. Scrambled eggs, with biscuits dripped in black berry jam filled our senses. Everything just tasted so much better on the beach and now was no exception.

Before we could say no, Victoria and I were seated beside the drifters, and played cards. A welcomed diversion; the casual atmosphere brought a sense of hope. These strangers really seemed to care what happened to us. But I was very wrong.

"I forgot to mention when the cards came out that everybody gives up something. It's part of the game knowing that you are willing to lose something." With that said, Marcos pulled his shirt off and threw it on the table. Sam laid his turquoise pocket knife right next to it. Pete opened up his wallet and took out a picture of a young girl and a teenage boy and placed it on the pile. "So tell me son, what are you willing to lose? What means the most to you?" Red alert rushed through me. Side tracked with idle kindness, we were set up. "And you little lady? What couldn't you do without?"

"This," at that exact moment, Victoria pulled out her kitchen knife and waved it back and forth. "You see it's very handy and being a chef I know just how to use it. In a presentation, the cuts are very important especially in Chinese Restaurants." The men's eyes were bigger than the crab's since they were not on stalks. Iced cement spoke. "Open the door." Nobody breathed but just stared at a mother and her cub. They were not prepared for a battle. The door flung open and just like that we walked. The tottering rig screeched down the road with burned rubber in its tracks.

"You know mom, we don't really know what's out here." Victoria lost all sense of bravado and collapsed in the sand.

"How long can I keep doing this? There is so little fight left in me. Is it worth it? I mean does it really matter if we make it or not?"

"Yes, it matters. That train will not leave without us." My pocket led us right where we needed to go. There was a crumbled-up train schedule just waiting to be found. Right about now the train was headed for Chicago. The train had berthed for the night so we really weren't so far behind. The race was on and we became Elmer's glue, inseparable.

THE WALK

So we walked, and walked. A shiny beige sports car pulled up beside us and a friendly young female voice told us to jump in. A contented baby wrapped in a white lined flannel blanket in the front seat cooed as we climbed in. Her little blond head twitched this way and that.

"You look like you could use some help. A long time ago, I was back there and somebody helped me." It was hard to imagine that this woman ever had a difficult time. Her large diamond ring flashed a blinding sign of success. "Few people empathize with the others, nobody even seems to see you and if they do they ignore you. Sometimes life just happens without your permission," Sandy gazed starry eyed at her baby." Victoria couldn't believe her ears; someone who walked through lack, and burst out on the other side.

"It's really not what you think. My husband got sick, couldn't pay the bills. We lost everything."

"It doesn't really matter what I think. You didn't lose everything. My little Mellie taught me that. As long as there was love, nothing else mattered. Then I met someone who agreed. You see it's not about what punched you down but that you stood up."

"My dad is comatose and can't move a muscle."

"Did it stop you?"

"No, it only destroyed me knowing that I couldn't change it."

"Nothing changed your love, did it?"

"No because I'm his son and stood up." Victoria's iced cement broke into little pieces. Sobbing relentlessly, she cried out.

"In an instant, I was evicted from my life. Without makeup, my friends couldn't even recognize me. The last few months I have worked and slept with terrorized people who spoke no English. In my left hand pocket, my kitchen knife has been my constant companion . . ."

"But what's in your heart?"

"Nothing." Victoria's cold battered rejection riveted through Sandy. The pit's bottom surfaced. CJ reached for his mother's hands and clasped them together.

"I'll revive your heart, beating joyfully again."

"Looks like you have something worth fighting for." Sandy turned up her classical music and drowned quickly in it.

"There is a train headed up north that we need to catch. We have family up there. Here's the train schedule." CJ paused as Sandy peered at the schedule.

"I know that train. We have traveled on it. I can get you to the next stop but not before we rest and eat." Within minutes Sandy pulled up to a Chinese Restaurant. Victoria winced and wouldn't budge.

CJ blurted out. "If possible, any other place other than this." Right down the road was a sign with a spinning steak on it. Before we knew it, steaks, salads, and desserts were piled up all around us. Hunger pounced.

Sandy gazed at this weary twosome whose eyes never connected with hers. She couldn't block the images: empty, lonely, desperate individuals. The men took care of themselves. But a mother and child tugged at her heart. In her wallet, Sandy's vacation money for Hawaii was still in the sealed envelope. Hawaii would just have to wait. Sandy scribbled 'for that joy,' and dropped the envelop into Victoria's empty pocket, the knifeless pocket. Victoria's attention was on her juicy steak and just assumed it was a couple of extra napkins.

As if covered in quicksand, everything within Victoria's grasp disappeared. Being full of steak, mashed potatoes, string beans, encrusted rolls, and fudge drizzled chocolate cake was a luxury to her shrived stomach There was something about a meal that you didn't have to prepare and serve.

Unexpected kindness seeped down into Victoria's soul. Her heart wanted to try again. She would take charge and let CJ be the thirteen–year old kid that he was.

Sandy beamed. Helping out was the best thing that happened to her in a very long time. Cares and concerns faded. A grateful thankfulness surged through her. Sandy had pushed her past so far behind that she forgot the lessons it left. Her shiny lifestyle would not be taken for granted.

The train would be easy to find. It was one of the few that went through this area. With time to spare, Sandy drove up to the station. CJ was horrified.

"Oh we forgot to tell you that we board the train in the back. We don't need a ticket."

"This trip you will be riding up front like everybody else. You will have a window to look out of and you won't miss a thing. You have plenty of money for train tickets and lodging and anything else that you will need for quite a while." Evidently Sandy knew something that we didn't. After tidying up in the rest rooms we looked like everybody else but our looks were not going to get us on that train.

"Have a good trip. Your mother will know what to do. Don't forget this, your trusted violin." And with that said, Sandy hesitated then pulled slowly out of the station. Our mouths opened and eyes widened as Victoria reached into her knifeless pocket, and pulled out the envelope.

"We didn't even have a chance to thank her."

"She didn't want any thanks. Angels you know."

Settled in the passenger seats wasn't nearly as fun. But in a very odd way, it was pleasant. Warm and safe, there was no worrying about men harassing Victoria. No thoughts about getting caught and thrown into jail. I began to enjoy the hills and white dotted houses with green shudders. We were not in the South any more. The colorful trees commanded our attention. Evergreen pine trees swayed this way and that. Most of the farms with red barns with fenced in cows and horses disappeared. Churches with white steeples and shiny crosses were shepherds that stood out in the hills watching below.

Just like at the movies, there were impeccably dressed porters who steered you here and there. When they realized that we really had tickets, It was kind of cool to have them wait on us. Not your typical passengers, Victoria collapsed and I squirmed around not wanting to miss a thing until the lady behind me suggested I visit the rest room. There was a car just for food. There was a car just to watch. There was a car just to sleep in. Bob, the porter sat down in an empty seat near us and told me all about the train. Being five inches from the ceiling, the top berths sounded more like confining bunk beds at camp. During the night, there were silent roll calls, berths were checked and rechecked. I already knew who they were looking for, the others. No longer labeled as one of them, I felt as if I cheated . The food from the menu was supposed to be from Grandma's kitchen. Never had a Grandma and mother used to be allergic to the kitchen. Bob cautioned me to keep my wallet hidden, something about out of sight out of mind. Since I didn't have a wallet, I forgot about what he said.

All kinds of passengers were on that train. Some blended in like wallpaper; others burst out like over-done popcorn. The attention grabbers were dressed with long pants and silky shirts. Oh and the shoes, pointed tasseled black loafers that clicked when they walked by. The air that they breathed was different. Their heads were high, their chest thrust forward and their gaits steady; there was no uncertainty about them. Their conversations confirmed it. They talked about business, and politics reminding me of the fathers that I used to know. But without the sports, it didn't remind me of my dad. Not a bit.

My violin case turned some heads, little heads then bigger heads. I opened the case and my fingers were drawn to the bow. Before I knew it, a well- practiced piece poured out of me. No longer on center stage, it sounded very different. The notes slurred together differently. With more effort, my bow glided with a mind of its own. Runaway tears shimmered down Victoria's cheeks. Surprisingly gratitude was passed forward, bills of different sizes and amounts. Conversation halted and ears opened. I guess I could quiet a train as well as an auditorium.

The thought suddenly occurred to me that I could be one of those street minstrels. Memories moved. Her flowing blond hair caught me off guard. Her flute music sung its own notes. Her purple dress danced as tucked in pink roses fell from her hair. A beautiful young girl could corral anyone. Her shiny flute case, stuffed full of money inspired me more than before.

"Didn't know you were so talented kid, looks can be deceiving. Where are the two of you actually headed?" questioned Bob.

"New York. Bet we will find a lot of work there."

"Yes, especially since you haven't finished middle school. You did say that you were thirteen. CJ, you will be surprised to know that there is actually a place called China Town in New York There are many open air markets with raw fish and vegetables."

"We will not be going there."

"Did you have gangs back at your school? In New York there are more. What you see will amaze you. Growing up in New York, I return every now and then. With so few apartments, rents are high. So cardboard is valuable up there; it's everywhere. On a busy day, if you stop on a sidewalk you can get run over. They say the people are colder up North because of the weather. But I think they are just plan tired from working so hard. In a week or so you will witness snow's first display and need warmer clothing. Do not be fooled by its beauty. It's deadly." Thank goodness Bob left. With such wonderful advice, we might as well turn around.

The afternoon passed quickly. In the dinner car, it was very odd having people wait on us as if we mattered. With tickets, we did. My music changed everything. Someone insisted on paying for our meal. When he saw the bil, he probably wished he hadn't since Victoria and I ordered enough for six people. My dad always used to tell me to eat slowly since my food wouldn't be taken away. His well-meaning words were no longer true.

At long last, we were alone in our confining berths. Once I got used to the top berth, it was more of an adventure rather than discomfort. I was an abandoned sardine without a can. Victoria didn't enjoy the adventure. Her longer legs craved space. There wasn't any.

"CJ, there was much more room back in the other car. Feel like moving?" Nervous, I made myself laugh. Victoria didn't. But as minutes went by, the discomfort calmed itself. The train's rocking was rhythmic and sleep held us.

Early the next morning I was up for a challenge. Being uneasy around strangers, I decided that this was a perfect opportunity to get easy around them. At breakfast I talked to people I never even used to look at. Each one had a unique story, some with half-healed heartaches. Victoria and I were not the only ones on the run.

The train screeched to a halt. 'Man overboard' was all that I heard. One of the others must have rolled out of the open train car. It wasn't a man at all but a fawn with some stubborn babies. They refused to get off the tracks and the conductor wasn't going to squish them. So there we were at a standstill.

Instinctively, I jumped down and walked slowly towards the babies. Knowing what it was like not to have a parent, I was determined that it would not be repeated. One of the fawns had some twine wrapped around its leg and was stuck. The others refused to move without him. Animals understood me. They were so much easier to fix than most of my peers. They didn't question or need to be convinced. The twine was dislodged and the fawn scampered quickly off the tracks. A loud roar sprang from the train. Only a kid would have cared enough, but that's what I was.

With all the unexpected attention, Victoria beamed. Our stop was next. For a brief moment we were connected, stitched together by time and circumstance. But oh so quickly that moment unraveled as soon as we stepped off the train.

THE GENTLE MAN

Getting this far was nothing less than miraculous. We hadn't even considered what our next plan was. As it turned out, Victoria did have a sister somewhere in New York. But where she actually lived was a mystery. The unlisted phone number had a plan of its own and disappeared.

As we trudged along, my violin case got heavier and heavier and Victoria got quieter and quieter. We were a ways from the city and one place was as good as another. We passed a quieter street with buildings stretched up way past the street lights. Big open windows peered back at us. Swaying back and forth, a sign read room for rent tossed itself in the wind. There was no reason not to stop.

With a bobbing nod and speckled beard, Mr. Simon greeted us. He spoke with an accent that was unfamiliar to me. His tasseled robe swished as his eyes hung lovingly on my face. Abruptly, confused tears slid down his face. Muttering forced words, his sorrow stopped us, another torn- up heart.

"Mr. Simon, what happened? What did I do?"

"He looked like you: handsome, young, full of life, charmed with his violin music. Did he send you?" Victoria pulled me closer.

"The sign outside said there was a room."

"Yes, Follow me. The room was on the second floor. The old radiator heater took up more space than allowed. Two small beds each covered with a matching faded bed spread waited to be slept in. A huge white porcelain pitcher rested on a small tabletop. Two un- sturdy chairs hovered under the patched curtains.

"This will do," I heard Victoria softly whisper.

"Fifty dollars a week, not a dollar more," quipped Mr. Simon's worn out recording. Victoria's face fell like the last autumn leaf from a cherished maple tree. The money, the envelope; it was gone. Her pocket was cut. During one of those nicer moments on the train someone stole it. Her sobs unglued both of us. In between sobs Victoria told how the young woman befriended us and gave us enough to last for a year or more. Mr. Simon said nothing as he shuffled back and forth.

"Fate will not be so kind to you next time. You are lucky that it was only the money that was stolen, nothing more. CJ will play the violin after dinner and fill this house with needed warmth. It will be enough."

What could have been a disaster was in fact a disguised delight. Mr. Simon was the grandfather I never had. Quite certain that he was somehow related, Victoria also fell in love with him. Every night, Mr. Simon read the Torah to us in Hebrew. At first the unaccustomed sounds hurt my ears but then my mouth started speaking them. Mr. Simon encouraged me to go deeper with my voice, guttural he said.

My violin poured out peace in the old man's heart. His heart ache rushed out.

"My wife had a bad habit of wandering off. When we lost our son, she just couldn't bear it. Every day she went out to look for him. Her heart left, then her mind. One day during a huge snowstorm she walked out and was frozen solid like a Popsicle. Struggling, I opened up the house to boarders. My emptiness subsided as I lost myself in others."

"Mr. Simon, what happened to your son?"

"What happened to many of us. Unbridled discrimination reared its ugly demented head."

"You mean your accent, the way you dress, your Hebrew?"

"Yes, being Jewish. I was a Rabbi at the temple. Some didn't want to hear our beliefs. Some didn't want us around. Some couldn't stand the very sight of us. My wife tried so hard to please, but I didn't. I just became more Jewish, spoke more Hebrew, spoke louder, prayed longer. Herron, my son took the brunt of it. One day after school, they ambushed him, a group of determined kids who wanted him gone. They were fed up with his good looks, his intelligence, his wit, his music, and his outspoken father. You see Herron reached out to the unbelievers; he loved and refused to hate. But the hate finally got him. When we found him a block away from the house, he was crumpled up, broken, destroyed. For a mere second, our voices brought him back. He opened up his eyes and told me he loved me, his Jewish father, his Jewish Rabbi. A moment later, he was gone forever and so were we."

Something rose up inside me. Then and there, I decided to take up Herron's quest: allowing love to cover hate.

Every night, Victoria's meals tasted better and disappeared faster. Every night my violin music soothed and medicated Mr. Simon's weary mind. His eyes trained me, coaxed me. When they suddenly opened, I was playing way too fast or without any passion. When his eyes closed, he drifted off hearing the familiar voices of long ago, hearing love. Mr. Simon taught me his beloved Jewish prayers and we accompanied them with music. Mixed with many sounds, my ears were filled with anguish, hope, and love.

With Mr. Simon's prompting, Victoria learned how to quilt. It was getting colder and custom quilts brought in good money. Looking for odd jobs in the neighborhood, I finally found one. A runner suited me. Here, the mail system didn't work really well so kids were hired to get packages to their destination. Christmas was quickly approaching and things got really hectic. Skinny and in good shape, I could cover a lot of ground. I was paid according to the number of packages I delivered. It challenged me.

"Hey CJ what happened to your shoes?" They were budding with holes. Just like a grandfather, Mr. Simon noticed everything.

"Oh, they're fine, just a little worn out. It's the style you know." That night there was a package for me, a brand-new pair of boots. Boots were foreign to me. In New Mexico, we didn't need them.

The next morning covered everything with snow, deep snow. Victoria couldn't wait to get out in it.

"Lie down and spread out your arms. I saw it in a movie once. I just looked at Victoria in disbelief.

"Why?"

"Snow angels." Overhearing, Mr. Simon suddenly appeared and showed me how it was done. Time faded. Once again, the three of us were little kids throwing all care to the snow. Mr. Simon's face glowed with steady warmth and his heart melted. His family never really left him after all.

At the time, we were the only borders which suited Mr. Simon just fine. It didn't make much sense to me since no money exchanged hands. But friendship did. Mr. Simon's character intrigued me. His most famous quote was,' it wasn't what a man thought that mattered, but what a man did.' In a round-about way, this quote led back to school. Mr. Simon's questions about history went unanswered and his math problems unsolved. Education was first and foremost on his mind.

By now I saved up enough money to pay him for almost all of our rent. So maybe it was time for that new season Mr. Simon always talked about. For all three of us, it was a new season but not one we would have chosen.

THE LETTER

The huge golden envelope, very noticeable, very official, was addressed to Mr. Simon. Government business, an immediate response was requested. A tightening coldness wrapped around my stomach. Unable to speak, my throat was a parched instrument. Just throw it away I thought, but that wasn't what Mr. Simon had drilled into my head. Reluctantly, I handed it over to his tasseled arm and watched the turbulent storm rush in. Whatever it was brought Mr. Simon to his knees. A washed with wailing, Mr. Simon cried out in desperation. Sinking to the floor, Mr. Simon's cool composure vanished completely like an early summer's fog on a hot summer day.

Victoria reached out and grabbed him. My feet were cast in quick sand. Witnessing Mr. Simon's sobs unnerved me more than my father's curled up legs. Bit by bit, the letter was read out loud. Something about back taxes, foreclosure, and the mortgage, grown-up stuff. But whatever it was destroyed Mr. Simon. Arm clinging to arm, Mr. Simon listened to Victoria's attempted Hebrew which stirred the air. Unglued, my feet sprung up as I grabbed the pillow case and emptied out my saved money for our unpaid rent. Clinging to me, Mr. Simon was a bear with his cub. Victoria's earnings from her quilt sales also appeared. With widened eyes, Mr. Simon observed us carefully. Softly, he sung his Hebrew prayers and quoted his beloved scripture.

"They can take whatever they want, but they can't take away my Jewish Lord, my faith, my obedience, born a Jew, always a Jew. There is nothing here for me now. It is time for me to return home."

"You're not going away forever, that wasn't what you meant was it? You can't just stop your life. You have taught me that it was a gift from God."

Selfishly, I couldn't imagine not serenading Mr. Simon with my violin, not eating oatmeal with him in the mornings, not praying in Hebrew whenever we wanted, and not telling him my inner most thoughts.

"CJ, I meant going back to Israel. It has always been just a matter of time. I will need a few weeks to get my things in order; it doesn't look like anything will be left. If I don't give the government what they want, they will throw me in jail and lose the key. I'm not about to wear an orange jump suit." Deep laughter burst out of us until we joined Mr. Simon on the floor in tears. The grandfather that I never had was taken away from me without permission, without any notice, without any delay.

"Couldn't we fight it? I could work harder; Victoria could sell more quilts."

"There are some things in life that aren't worth fighting CJ, the government is one of them. In all honesty, I expected this letter for a long time. As you can see the house is really in bad shape. The roof should have collapsed with all of the heavy snow."

When you wanted time to slow down it hurried all the faster. For the longest time, it wasn't about Victoria and me. All of our energy went into helping Mr. Simon, being his hands and feet. Within days, men in pressed suits arrived. They were determined but unable to find very much. We had just enough time to get Mr. Simon's valuables packed up and stowed in my locker at the post office. Driven the men had their way and a big condemned sign was posted on the front porch's awning. Our joy shriveled up like a forgotten piece of choice fruit that dried up when it toppled outside a stuffed picnic basket.

With the last good bye, Mr. Simon's frozen face peered out at us from the cab's splotchy window. His departing words whispered into my ears. "Life is about change. You have to be willing to let things go or you will not survive. Don't be distracted by the world or allow your heart to be taken in." The taxi sped away. His words of encouragement were gusts in the wind suddenly gone.

THE STREETS

My violin case was heavy in hand. Victoria's face was a glazed over ice pond, still, quiet, unresponsive. With two light packed bags and two needed quilts, we trudged down the sidewalk with emptiness. I mourned the loss of the grandfather that I never had. Knowing that I would never see Mr. Simon again, I already missed the early morning encouragement over hot oatmeal and raisins. Our nightly ritual of Hebrew prayers and psalms were locked inside of me. When I learned enough Hebrew, Mr. Simon gave me his skull cap. It was tucked carefully away in my belongings. If I ever sat down to a dinner again, it would be on my head. So I guess in a way, he was still with me.

Even with mittens, my hands were pricked cold. Victoria was bundled up like the abominable snow woman. As I tucked my hands deep into my pockets, I clutched the small wallet that Mr. Simon insisted that I take. I was the guardian; it was not to leave my sight. There was enough money for food, and a room for at least a few weeks. My legs were much colder walking than my usual running. Victoria lagged behind so I slowed down. There were no words only the sound of softly crunching boots in the endless snow. The quietness strolled away as the noise of the city approached us.

The sidewalks were chocked full of life: Men and women scurried for their lives. Jagged jaws were set in stone: not seeing, not hearing as if on remote control. Eyes straight ahead glued to the horizon. Did they even see what was around them? Cardboard boxes that breathed. Feet stuck out every which way. Hands reached out for anything. A little girl's voice moaned.

"Please mister, I haven't eaten for two days. My stomach hurts." A ten- dollar bill flew out of my hands. Two pigtails wrapped around a younger brother scurried down the street for the hot dog and pretzel stand. The doughy salty pretzels were a meal in itself. The hotdogs were an afterthought. Victoria's eyes were blinded with tears. I could hear her thoughts. Victoria sensed that a sidewalk spot was reserved for her and CJ. Walk-ins were welcome. No reservations were required. She and her son were not going to inhale cardboard. Regardless of what she had to do, the sidewalk was not going to be her front door.

She missed Mr. Simon, the old man, his fatherly ways and wisps of wisdom. Mr. Simon's love was endless, a carafe of warm maple syrup that just oozed out. How in the world would she or CJ be expected to survive without his guidance? CJ blossomed in Mr. Simon's care. So had she. She was so pleased with everything CJ did, his resilience, his awareness of others. He was not the same son that fell completely apart when their house was torn out of their grasp.

CJ stopped listening. He needed to come up with some kind of a plan. Surely there had to be some lodging near here. Victoria got slower and slower and the snow swirled faster and faster. He spied a neon sign that shouted out. Turning off the road, they stumbled into a quaint inn bustling with activity. There were two restaurants, for the haves and the have nots. People checked in as others checked out. There wasn't much of a wait as the owner studied us.

"There's hot water upstairs and plenty of heat. Breakfast every morning; A fire stoked in the fireplace every evening. There is a small burner to heat up soup and hot chocolate. The rest is up to you. Looks like the two of you could use some quiet, some rest; you will find it here. We are in the city limits but not in the center of town. It will be seventy-five dollars a week for both of you." He paused and waited. I was the man in charge now and took the money out of my wallet and paid the fee. The owner, Mr. Ping, looked at me in surprise and taped me on the head. "Good for you, son. Take care of her." I felt Mr. Simon's smile a thousand miles away. This was just the first smile of many.

The bed was clean and springy. My check for bed mites began. Mr. Simon's cautious advice. That night Vitoria coughed and coughed and coughed as though her life depended upon it. There was a pan of hot water billowing out steam on one of the burners. Victoria sat in front of it and breathed heavily. The cold almost claimed her.

In the morning, there was a knock on the door. Mr. Ping called a doctor. During the night, Victoria's coughs echoed down the air shafts. People left early not wanting to catch it, since this was the season for the dreaded flu.

The doctor looked, searched, and checked. Lumps of swollen red tissue blocked her throat. The doctor's face winced as though he felt the restricted breathing.

"Complete and utter bedrest or you will utterly collapse. Your lungs can't take much more of this." A chilled spasm radiated throughout my body. Victoria was all that I had left in the world. I wasn't going through this alone. It was both of us or neither of us.

"Your advice will be followed, I spoke determinedly." Victoria didn't have much spunk and sank back completely exhausted.

"Son you will have to sleep on that makeshift couch and breathe circulated air. You need to stay out of this room as much as possible." The doctor handed me a face mask, the kind they wore during an operation. Under the mask was the fee. My face paled. It was almost as much as a week's rent. Having no other choice, I reluctantly counted out the bills and made my fingers give them to the doctor. The doctor's heart hesitated. "Here son, you need this more than I do." Returning most of it, the doctor reached in his bag and gave me a bottle of cough medicine and enough antibiotics for more than a week. "Samples son, always come in handy. You must be vigilant and make sure your mother stays warm and still." Carrying a heavy burden, the guilty doctor quickly turned as a stray tear streaked down his cheek remembering his own wife that he lost not so long ago because he was too busy to take care of her.

Outside, things also quickly changed. During the night ten inches of snow fell. From the window, it looked harmless enough but it wasn't. Cars screeched up and down the street as truckloads of sand squirted across the road. The first storm of the season showed its vengeance. Mr. Ping's snow shovel felt right at home in my hands. His walks needed shoveling. It was a day to make some needed money. The hot plate was only good for steam. Victoria needed healthy food, restaurant food, expensive food.

There was a rhythm to the shoveling: breathe in, dig in, lift up, and hurl with all your might A frantic voice cried out, "Look out its coming right at you." Somehow intense supernatural energy rushed through me as I jumped clear of the out of control, spinning car. Hitting a patch of ice, the runaway car careened off the road and brushed my coat as it squealed by me. Landing in a huge snow bank, the very stretched out car needed to be rescued and dug out. It was a $200.00 blessing in disguise. My arms ached but I kept on digging and sweating. Funny how I sweated as much under a sweater and coat in fifteen-degree weather as I did in a strenuous basketball game. Mr. Ping assured me that it was very normal and that it wasn't a symptom of the dreaded flu.

Age had its benefits. Because of my smaller size I could get into places with that shovel that others couldn't. After a few hours of toil, the car was freed. It had been a long time since I saw such relieved faces. Hat in hand, a very dressed up man climbed into the driver's seat. The stressed-out husband handed me his card and told me if I ever needed anything to give him a call. Did he know what those words really meant? He was from a distant world, as his stylish wife urged him to get his driver back on the road. The card slid out of my hand into the slushy snow. I kicked it around and then reluctantly picked it up and thought nothing about it.

The sun sank quickly into the horizon as I finished up the last walk. The sky was ablaze with pinks, purples, and golds. Being outside was much more invigorating than looking at four walls, especially walls coated with the flu. Part of me wanted to go up to check on Victoria and part of me didn't. I cleared my throat; it still worked. Mr. Ping gave me a portable fan that helped move the air around. Two hot plates of goulash, a stew of some kind, and plenty of hot buttered bread with a quart of milk were delivered to our room. As if in hibernation, Victoria came slowly to life before my very eyes.

Chilly was hardly the word. The window pane had icicles hanging all over it. What did the cardboard box people do in this cold? Little did I know that I would soon find out the answers to my question.

As the week trudged on, Victoria emerged out of her medicine induced trance. I didn't really know who I was happier for my mother or myself. She started breathing without the cough medicine. Sounds of desperation faded.

At night, there was a bright lit store whose sign glowed. Victoria needed some warmer lined street clothes. Sickness was unaffordable. Though it wasn't Christmas yet, it looked like a Christmas past. Bags were stuffed with sweaters, pants and just about everything from the store, including sweets: red, green, and white ribbon candy twisted and melted in our mouths. Victoria's eyes were lit up fires, pouring out unexpected warmth. For that one brief moment I didn't care how much money I spent. The very next day I did.

Mr. Ping took me aside and told me that the Christmas' room rates were now in effect. There wasn't enough money to stay one more night. Toting my violin, I breathed in heavily and Victoria breathed out easily. The streets silently welcomed us back.

CHOICELESS

This time was different. Victoria and I were healthy, well-fed, warmly dressed, and broke. Once again snowflakes attached themselves to bigger flakes and stuck on everything except our faces since warm hats and face masks covered us. The weather changed everything. It didn't care if you struggled or what you thought. Why would anyone live in a place like this? Maybe others like us were just stuck here.

Victoria's thoughts collided with mine. Up until now, things were tolerable. Even with her sickness, Victoria knew that her lungs would heal. But this weather was vicious, taking casualties whenever it could. She and her son were not going to be taken down. CJ's resourceful nature steered them this far. But there were limitations, with no boundaries.

Steam wafted from a nearby vent. Other arms and legs huddled around the surging warmth which invited us in. Alarmed, Victoria saw others who were starving, destitute, and ready to give up. In the far corner, there was a man giving away cardboard boxes. "We could always get one and then give it to someone else," quipped Victoria. She refused to admit what she really meant. The vent threw out untouched steaming heat.

"Lady you and the lad might need one of these before the night's out. Might as well take it."

"Where does all this heat come from?" I asked. "From the subways, there are tunnels underground and all this heat just pours out of them. At night, the makeshift boxes encircle these vents. They are invisible to others and are ignored by all. It is just a way of life here for the cold, the forgotten, the have-nots, for us. Victoria pulled CJ back. She and CJ were not in that category nor would they ever be. This was just a trying time to get through and tomorrow was another day. Her desperate thoughts were not allowed to breathe. She fought them at night.

In the distance, CJ spied an open park, a cold winter wonderland. He saw some beautiful chestnut brown horses with white prancing feet pulling fancy drawn carts driven by a top hat driver. He grabbed Victoria's hand and headed in their direction. There was too much daylight to worry about tonight.

The horses were smitten. CJ's love for animals burst out. He still had some left-over peanuts from the steamed vent gathering, high in protein supposedly all you needed for the night. The winnowing horses couldn't crunch them fast enough.

The top hat spoke. "How about a ride for you and the lady? Everything in me said yes, but everything in my wallet said no. "How about a dollar a piece? You know it's almost Christmas, the special rates begin. These horses need the exercise after all of those peanuts." Victoria was already nestled in the sleigh under the heavy blanket. Before anything changed anyone's mind, we were off.

From his thermos, Thomas poured out two steaming cups of hot chocolate and unwrapped numerous chocolate chip cookies. "You know, sometimes things are not quite what they seem. For instance, take this park. In the late afternoon, it's beauty is overwhelming. The red tailed squirrels scurrying here and there. The male cardinals dressed in bright red coats and black caps over shadow their mates, the blended-in brown females. The kids skating on the pond all dressed up in their winter best. Families hand in hand singing carols with all the gusto of the season. But once the sun goes down the beauty fades. Desperation doesn't hide its face. The lost come out. They blend in with the darkness. Remember no matter what, you don't want to be in this park after dark, for any reason." Agreeing, the horses whinnied. "But right now just sit back and relax and enjoy the Christmas carols."

Throughout the park, loud speakers piped out some beautiful melodies. My violin case popped open. Frozen fingers played. I played for the well-dressed kids skating on the pond, the ragged children in the cardboard boxes, Mr. Simon who was now safely back In Israel, and for my dad wherever he was, looking down from above or trapped in tortured muscle spasms. Then I played for me. A sense of delightful peace sunk in. Victoria gave me that look of hers, that look of wonder, that look that she wouldn't want to be anywhere else but right here with me and the horses and top hat Thomas.

Clumps of snow were winter quilts that clung to the evergeen pine trees. Bright red berries hung on the leafless vines. One by one, the birds swooped in. Blue jays bluer than the patched sky shrieked as they came in for a landing. Their fluttering wings made it all look so easy, so effortless.

"Mighty fine music lad." In case you need a place to stay, there are always the tunnels. There are only certain ways to get there and someone has to invite you down. The rules are stricter below than above. If they don't like you, you don't stay. There are no second chances there. Often you don't make it out alive. But if it gets too cold, ask for Mr. Clang, the tunnel escort. Someone will take you to him. Tell him Thomas from the park sent you." Thomas had a cold faraway look in his eye. I watched his face change and his thoughts. He wished he could help those in the tunnels. Yet as it were he barely made it out alive. His mind was dragged back to the tunnels.

The dirty fingers examined him. His pockets were emptied for him. Everything you had belonged to everyone. His frostbite was unbearable. Like a runaway snowball, the tunnel's warmth hit him in the face. Then there was the interrogation, the questions. There were no answers. He was given a heated bowl of soup, a weathered blanket and a visitor's cubicle, a dug out area which no one else wanted. In the morning he was expected to bring in anything: thrown out food, garbage, or discarded items on the streets. It was his entrance fee for the next night. He slept uneasily knowing at any moment he could be knifed, shot, or smothered for no reason at all. A present gust of wind brought him back to his senses.

"CJ take this for protection." It was a pocket knife some forgotten stranger had given him years ago when he really needed it. "Hide it and don't show it to anyone no matter what the circumstance. Don't let fear uncover it." Victoria was thankful for Thomas' interest in her son. Wanting her son to fully enjoy the warmth when all that awaited them was dark and uncertain.

When the sun left the sky, the frigid cold jumped in. Hot chocolate, cookies and a pocket knife were not enough to keep them warm. By now the makeshift parking lot around the steam vents overflowed with huddled bodies mostly in boxes or tattered blankets. A line of continued cardboard kept the area clear of snow. Small fires in trash cans were lit and relit. The police strolled by and warned us to get off the streets. They hollered, spit, and swore, then left. It was all quite a show.

Tunnels were for rats and mice or so I thought. If I were by myself, maybe I would have stayed on the street. This was no place for mothers. Mothers were not supposed to see things like this. It was all a bad documentary about the worst of the worst, 'What to do when you had nothing.' One way or another, we had to get into the tunnels. When I mentioned Mr. Clang's name, loosened teeth were spit out, clutched fists raged into the air, and words that I never even heard spewed out of mouths, a volcanic eruption of hatred. I didn't care. Mr. Clang's tunnels were our destination.

There were only a few covered stairwells that led into the dreaded tunnels. With a mere dollar, I persuaded a tattered figure to pry open the sewer head and announce us. It was far from a royal summoning. The jabbering stopped and we were allowed entrance. Black as pitch was an understatement. Victoria was exhausted and just hung on to my coat. The humid warmth was suffocating. A loud demanding voice took over.

"Leave them here. We're full up for he night." Our guide couldn't get out fast enough. My breath left me as my mouth cracked. Speaking instinctively, I muttered, Thomas sent us."

"Oh that changes everything. Is that what you think boy? Thomas barely made it out of here alive. Should you be allowed to live, you and the other?" as he pointed to Victoria who just collapsed on the warmed cement. Allowed to live, was this guy kidding.

"I don't care who you are or who you aren't. We are frozen and won't leave. Give me a blanket and leave us alone."

"You've got spunk kid, I like that. I'm not at all interested in either one of you. You are pitiless just like all the rest of them." With that said, he threw a blanket at me and vanished. No one was around us; I kicked every hole, every duct, every mound of dirt. Nothing moved. The saturating warmth seeped into our clothes, our hands, or legs, our souls. It was shelter for the night, out of the biting cold into warmed uncertainty.

Early, a small voice woke me up. "Hot oatmeal?" It was a kid, a small kid. Before I could reply, two heaping bowls arrived. "Eat quickly before the others waken, they will fight you for it. It's Eric, I'm off to school. They won't let us in if we're late. If you made it through the night, you already passed the initiation. Welcome to the tunnels." With that said, Eric disappeared as quickly as our oatmeal. As frozen dreams thawed, Victoria was lulled back to sleep.

The lights at the end of the tunnel needed explanation. I mean we're underground, weren't we? Being pretty sure of myself, I crouched down as I explored the tunnel. I stumbled and fell just as two figures came into view. Pulling my legs out of view I pretended to be asleep.

"What's that kid doing there so late? He must have already dropped out of school like the rest of us. Need to get him a pipe; might as well learn how the rest of us survive." A sweet suffocating smell caused my chest to burn. I could hardly breathe. Hearing nothing, I walked towards the light. Stilled figures smoked and stared into space. Dead men breathing. Every which way, they were all marked up with tattoos even in their scalps. One draped figure stuck a shiny needle in his forearm as a raged tourniquet fell to the ground. This was a drug zone from outer limits. It was the wrong place. It was too late.

"Where do you think you're going kid? He's seen too much already. Here give him some of this; it's already been mixed." Everything stopped. Nobody breathed.

"Let him go; he's a visitor. The voice didn't ask; it commanded. The disturbed men quickly left. "This is off bounds for you." His metallic silver streaked hair bounced off the light. His rugged furrowed brow was a sailor's profile off the boat. He studied me and lead me back down the tunnel.

"Here like at school, we follow the rules. Nobody breaks them including the kids. If they are broken, there are consequences. You are erased like a cleaned up black board. By the way, they call me Master Clang."

"So they are your slaves?"

"They do what I say."

"I am nobody's slave."

"That's why you're still breathing. Daily chores. When the sun heats things up we go out. Thrown out food, clothing, anything nobody wants we use. Down here, there is no mine. It is team work."

"So we're all on the same team?"

"More or less, except for the leaders. It is my job to protect you from the others."

"You mean those walking on the streets, the employed, the fed, the clothed, the prosperous? Those who sleep in beds, own apartments, aren't you a little confused? You should be protecting me from you. See I'm not afraid of you. You're nothing but an uneducated bully with metallic hair."

"Enough, enough nobody talks to me that way. You will keep your thoughts silent. Are you warm, are you alive? Enough said, Who is with you? Do you care what happens to her? The men down here are hungry for companionship." Raw anger, pure hatred, a deep volcano exploded from miles within.

"If you or anyone else even looks in her direction I will kill you."

"I believe you would. Just know that rebels don't survive in tunnels." I no longer cared about anything this ignorant bully had to say.

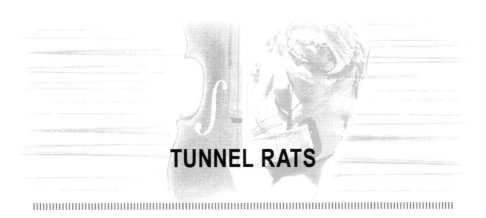

TUNNEL RATS

B efore we emerged, we hid our belongings and violin case under a deep pile of loosened boards. Victoria and I couldn't get out of the tunnel fast enough. The thought of going through the rubbish bins for food gaged me. The underground men were living germs; they were the walking dead. There was enough money left for Victoria and me to eat, maybe a hot dog a day. The sun felt clean, warm and revealing.

"Victoria, here's the plan. If we get back late enough, there won't be anyone to check and see what we have donated for the lodging experience. The losers down there don't even know day from night. Take this knife and always keep your distance from the rest of them. There were no other women down there. At night, keep your hair pulled back and scrunch up your face. The worse you look the better off you will be."

"CJ, that timid wisp of a mother stayed back in New Mexico. For now, we will just have to put up with their nonsense. Warmth has its price. I need to find something to do while you're at school."

"School, are you kidding?"

"Do you really think that I am going to let you turn out like those lost hopeless men? School tomorrow, just follow Eric and the other kids and get there." I knew Victoria was right; five long months had passed.

Victoria and I lost ourselves on the streets watching people watch us. By now, we were a little shabby and dirty, not our dry clean best. Public rest rooms caught my eye. Victoria went one way and I went the other. It was amazing what paper towels, soap, water, and a comb could do. Water was free and I drank my fill. Victoria surprised me with a glowing face, brushed hair, even a little make up. Mother looked better than her old self. Her confidence danced. Amazing what a tunnel could do.

"Son, during the day we will look our best, like the others. Those clothes need to be changed before tomorrow." Once a mother, always a mother. Victoria's undisclosed quilting money burst out of hiding. An inexpensive store taunted us. Two new pairs of jeans, three flannel shirts, and three pairs of heavy socks, were placed in a bag with my name on it. "Tomorrow, you will blend in with the other boys." Time changed everything. I couldn't even remember what my cool clothes looked like. Nor did I care. My appearance no longer defined me.

It was our last day together for many days, a celebration of sorts knowing that even the freezing determined streets couldn't destroy us. The day flew by on eagles' wings; sensing a new beginning, we both soared. Our old tattered relationship of mother and son broke into a thousand shattered pieces. In its place, stood respect, admiration, and flexibility.

A brief foot tour of Manhattan revealed hungry pigeons that flashed green and grey feathers from their fluttering wings. From the harbor you could see the Stature of Liberty, the torch of possibility. The heated bus was a welcome change. Blending in, we looked like everyone else, on a mission, but with nowhere to go.

The snow stopped for a brief intermission. Dazzling, the white was blinding. Whatever winter wore, you respected it. Transparent ice blocked much of the river. The free running water sparkled towards the middle. Everywhere, Icicles were hung curtains that opened momentarily with the sun's heat.

The clang of Red Cross bells and red buckets lined every corner. So many people, so many needs and wants. Competing with one another, the shop windows and doors donned Christmas wreaths and fancy strung up bells. Five months ago I would have missed it, too many distractions, who I was and what I had. Today, simple joy rushed through me; what I didn't have made me so content. Leaving my contented mark, I kissed mother on the cheek.

"Victoria, I'm glad that everything changed. I never would have met my best friend." Victoria's eyes fogged over and joy, a swollen balloon, burst. "CJ, You're still going to school tomorrow."

That crowded bus took us around and around. There was so much of the city to see that we just never got off until after dark. Dinner, partly opened bags of potato chips, was found under one of the seats. Warmed, tired and fed we were the last ones off, a completed circle right back where we started from.

By now the restroom's warmed cubicles were jammed. Sinks were stopped up with water and hair was being washed. Soap was everywhere, kids were cleaned up and scrubbed like washboards. Looking around, the fathers were desperate. Hungry and cold, they wanted more, they had to find more for their children. The trash cans were emptied and picked through. The cemented electric hand driers dried the wet locks and children were bundled back up for the cold. Water bottles were filled and shifts changed.

Families out, singles in. The older single men didn't move so fast. Toothless grimaces sneered at me.

"Brush your teeth while you still have them." Overstaying my welcome, I couldn't help but stare; it was just so surreal. Once it slowed down, I washed my own hair with gooey strawberry hand soap that smelled like a toilet brush, changed clothes, and gave myself a pep talk. Without hair goop, wholly fashion jeans, and two hundred dollar sneakers, I wouldn't be a social distraction at any school. The teachers wouldn't even look at me. Instead of fooling around, I planned to really listen, to learn.

Finally, Victoria appeared without a trace of makeup. She smudged some grey stuff under her eyes and looked horrible.

"You look great mom. You might even hurt some eyes." Victoria was ready for the tunnel which wasn't too far away. Shoving the sewer lid this way and that, it got stuck. Underneath, one of the kids heard me banging on the lid and pushed it up.

"Quickly, before you're noticed. Go back to the same spot where you were yesterday. At seven o'clock, we leave for school." The area was completely swept and picked up, two blankets and two wicked lamps sat in the corner, waiting. The pile of loosened boards was arranged a little neater. Our stuff hadn't been found. It was even warmer than last night and no sign of any greeters. Fear fled. Sleep triumphed.

SCHOOL AGAIN

Nothing like my old school, but school was school, a building, classes, teachers and kids. Down the street, Eric and the other kids attended middle school. Ninth grade seemed so grown up; but it was really I who had grown up. Nobody looked twice at me which was expected. Nobody really asked me much except the counselors who were used to kids like me. "No home, no problem," seemed to be the silent moto. If you were smart, everything else was overlooked.

Surprisingly, I still had it. Manhattan High seemed more difficult than my last school. Since the counselor put me in advanced courses, the classes were smaller. The kids were smart and very competitive. They just wanted to know what you knew. If you didn't know anything they ignored you.

The interracial mixture even carried over to the teachers which made it much more interesting. My catching glove wasn't missed. But my violin was. Music was everywhere. Jazz was the thing here. Then I remembered I was homeless. They wouldn't want to jam with a tunnel kid. I was determined that no one would ever know.

Lunch was humbling. Famished, I just glanced at what I couldn't afford. Then a food fight erupted and food was hurled everywhere. I had to sit on my hands so I wouldn't gobble down the ammunition. If they only knew what they were throwing away. There should be a law. There was. Decorated with hanging noodles, sauces, and butterscotch pudding, many were escorted down to the principal's office. No one expected to see those kids again anytime soon.

The cool kids didn't say too much, but when they spoke everyone listened very closely. I should have listened better. There was something that you just never did, you never went to the bathroom alone, only with groups of kids. I found out the hard way. The restrooms were older in fact the whole building was about 100 years old which was very cool. As I took a second look in the bathroom's mirror, a group of guys wandered in. "He's not here. But what about that kid?" A pack of restroom wolves, they surrounded me and sniffed. "Don't waste your time. No money on that kid. Check out the hair. Strawberry fields forever." Some blades flashed and I threw up all over the floor. They left none too soon. Mr. Restin, my math teacher just appeared and confessed.

"CJ you can't come in here by yourself; it isn't safe. You have to stay away from the packs of kids. In the regular classes, there are tougher kids, delinquents who have done community service. They don't like the smarter kids; they rarely interact. Never let your classmates out of your sight, especially the guys. It will prove to be invaluable. Some kids don't ever make it out of the rest rooms."

"You mean without being jumped or hit?"

"No I mean on a stretcher given up for dead. This is New York, lots of gangs and hatred. The only way out is intellect and that you have. Make friends with the musical kids; they are the ones going places. Guess you missed your bus by now?"

"No, I walk, the wind clears my head."

"Don't forget your assignments. It is the only way to stay in your advanced classes." Eric and the others gathered down at the end of the street.

"What took you so long? We were just about to leave." These kids were a pack in themselves. NO lone wolfs here. No one did anything alone.

"Hey Eric, where are all the parents?" Not a word.

"There aren't any. These kids are runaways, misfits, the unwanted, the others, rejects. When they left, nobody looked. The streets gobbled them up. In the tunnel, they are safe from predators unless they are snootingly handsome, you know like in the magazines. But kids like that aren't like us. They have families no matter how mixed up they are."

"In our lives, the older kids fill in as parents. You would be almost a grandfather, I guess. We don't put any importance on family, just on the group. We try to help each other out, to grow up and get beyond sixteen. Disease, drugs and alcohol finish a lot of us off. One by one we disappear. One day we are there, and the next day we aren't. Nobody asks any questions; there are never any answers. They tell us that things will change, but they never do. Mr. Clang promises. Talk goes just so far."

"Do you really think that guy cares about what happens to you? Stop picking through the trash and pickpocketing and see how fast he throws you out. He only wants what he can get out of you."

"You're right. I run drugs for him. Get the cash, make the exchange and deliver the merchandise."

"And you think that's right, getting people hooked on drugs?"

"I don't know. I never thought about it. There's no right here. I don't know what's right. Only that I survive." I felt so badly for Eric and the rest of the kids. They had absolutely nothing, not even a conscience. Half of their lives were already gone. They needed help, there had to be a way out. I didn't return with the kids. Clear thinking was needed.

There was a little coffee shop with obscure metal tables surrounded with fake plants. The change I had was just enough for a hot chocolate. It was a perfect place for homework. The owner didn't seem to care how long I stayed since there were so few customers. Instinctively I cleared a few of the tables so I wouldn't have to look at the clutter. Someone left half of a ham and cheese sandwich so I inhaled it. A perfect solution to my hunger, better than the garbage cans along the streets.

Victoria and I met up by the park. The sun was sinking and the air chilled. When she saw my face her heart skipped many beats. A huge sigh of relief saturated the air. Being alone was foreign to both of us. We hadn't been separated since the house was repossessed. Couldn't wait to tell her about my day. It was so nice to be around smart kids who were my own age.

Victoria saw the new light in her son. She made the right decision. School was not an if any more. CJ beamed with confidence as he showed her his finished assignments. Victoria would keep herself busy with anything. There was a way to work these streets. People wanted to be waited on. Maybe the shoe shiner or pretzel wagon could use another pair of hands.

Once back in the creepy tunnel, the kids insisted that CJ play his violin. CJ needed to start practicing if he were going to impress the school musicians. The beautiful notes just sprung out of him. Hesitating, he remembered his promise to Mr. Simon and placed his Yamaha on his head. Now he felt the notes and the rhythm. Mr. Simon's eyes closed with joy. The violin stirred something deep inside.

The beautiful music captured hearts inside and outside the tunnel. The music couldn't be contained. People stopped and couldn't figure out where the music was coming from. After a while, there was quite a crowd despite the cold frigid air. People lingered, cried, and then just felt better. The sounds of cheering reverberated through the tunnel.

The next day it was all over the papers. Victoria couldn't help but see the headlines as she passed by the news stand.

"Yes sir that created quite a stir heard it myself. It was as if heaven opened up under ground; the most riveting music Then after a while it just stopped. Someone said it had to come from the subway; it was music that seeped out of the ground."

As if she had run a marathon, a deep overwhelming pride ran all through her. Her son could melt hearts inside a packed auditorium or inside a deserted homeless tunnel.

Cj carried his violin to school and couldn't wait for the string jam during lunch. But it was jazz and he was all classical. But why not put the two together and so they did. This kid Bert on a viola befriended him. They were two musical soccer balls that bounced off one another and lit up the field. After school, Bert insisted that he take CJ to some of his hangouts. Music was everywhere. Instruments made out of barrels with strings, drums that hummed and wooden flutes that ached and sighed Bert was very cool and asked me nothing. He just wanted to show me off to his friends. When they picked up their instruments all heads turned and all mouths stopped. For the first time in a long time, I felt home. Where I slept didn't matter, what I ate didn't matter, what I wore didn't matter. Despite all of it, my spirit soared higher and higher. I was so thankful that my violin played out its heart; we were again inseparable.

Later that day, Victoria surprised me with the article from the paper. Maybe there was a way out of this tunnel. Seeing possibility, we laughed until we cried knowing full well that there was always hope even in a desperate tunnel full of drug addicts and alcoholics. A breath of chance stirred the air.

ON GUARD

My favorite class turned out to be gym. Since after dark there wasn't much room in the tunnel, the gym was an oasis. The showers were an added bonus with rich lathery soap, and real shampoo for your hair. It was a delight to take my time so unlike the public restrooms where others would just assume trample you as wait. Being so clean, I cringed putting my dirty clothes back on.

Bert read my mind and surprised me with an assorted bag of clothes he no longer needed.

"CJ try these on, I don't wear them much anymore. You will need some jazzy clothes for the afternoon gigs coming up. It's better when we match more or less." I couldn't wait to match. But there was something else he wanted to tell me but didn't.

Meanwhile through trial and error, Victoria learned what was expected as a resident and what wasn't. Surviving in a tunnel was kind of like renting a room, things you did and things you didn't. Now that CJ was a thriving student, her day was her own and needed to be filled. She made it a point to leave right after CJ One morning she didn't.

Victoria was sound asleep and something poked at her.

"Get up. Breakfast needs to be made." An interrupted dream. Pushed down the tunnel, there was a makeshift kitchen: a hot plate, a small refrigerator and something that looked close to a table made out of bricks and a board. Surprisingly the refrigerator was full of food: eggs, meat, fruits and milk. It was hooked up to a generator that whirled a tune of its own. Eggs were on the menu and she fixed them. Before their plates were cleaned, a hand reached up grabbed her arm and yanked her down. A blood curdling scream echoed throughout the tunnel. Victoria's free hand reached within her pocket and flipped the knife's blade. She lashed out at anything and everything. Within seconds the room emptied as plates rolled any which way. Victoria's adrenalin gave way as she collapsed into a chair

A commanding voice announced. "So you have met the boys. You shouldn't be too surprised you are the only female down here. Pretty much tried to tell your son that." With every bit of gumption, she could muster, Victoria pulled herself up and commanded Mr. Clang's undivided attention.

"Your words mean absolutely nothing to me. You are no different." She pulled the blade out and swiped it toward Mr. Clang. Just in the nick of time, he jumped back, spat on the ground, and proclaimed, "You aren't even a woman," and disappeared. Victoria knew all too well her womanhood would not survive another attack. Victoria pushed the gruesome scene out of her mind and quickly pushed up the tunnel's lid. Thinking about what just happened made her sick.

Once out in the morning air her chilled thinking cleared. Work, where could it be? The other day, the pretzel man actually winked at her. Was it her splotchy makeup; or something else? Within an hour, she was roasting salted pretzels, gabbing with New Yorkers and feeling like part of the action. People were people whether they lived in pent houses or cardboard boxes. Everyone got hungry and even in the morning everyone like gooey twisted salted pretzels. It was refreshing: listening, sharing, gossiping; shades of her old life burst through. She chuckled to herself-imagining an outing with one of these fine gentlemen, to be picked up at the tunnel's lid. Laughing hysterically, she only sold more pretzels. Whether a business man or a bum, everyone could use some laughter.

"You're just what we needed out in this cold," proclaimed Mr. Sets. Where does it all come from?"

"You have no idea." Once again, Victoria felt human, felt like she mattered somehow in the middle of all of this mess. By the pretzel's heater, It was toasty warm. Then it happened. From the corner of her eye, one of her friends from Victoria's old comfortable past came into view. With her makeup intact, Victoria felt confident almost like her old self. All bundled up in coats everyone looked pretty much the same. Out here, what was under the coat no longer mattered.

"Victoria whatever are you doing here?" Delia's grin exploded.

"Oh, I thought that I would try something new."

"But you hate to cook."

"Not anymore."

"Things also changed for me, I am now divorced and live here in New York. Paul just got up one morning and never came home. I was served with papers. After twenty years of marriage, not even one courteous phone call. At the hearing Paul was accompanied by a younger woman who couldn't keep her hands off of him. With absolutely no eye contact, our relationship was merely a smoke screen that finally lifted with time. For Paul, I no longer existed What about you?"

For the very first time in a long time, Victoria felt no shame at all about her past. "We lost the house and everything in it. My husband also left me but not by choice. Disease mangled and kidnapped his body. CJ and I had to make a new life for ourselves." Victoria thought about inviting Delia for tea in the tunnel but thought better of it. Unmistakable tears rushed into Delia's eyes. Delia's glove hand reached out and hung on to Victoria's.

"Don't forget too much." With that said, she was gone. Victoria felt strangely comforted knowing that Delia also changed and forgot things that were important to her. A new courage rushed through Victoria. Hot pretzels today, what about tomorrow? Victoria tucked Delia's address into her coat pocket. Without permission, life had taken both their loved ones. Change didn't wait for anyone.

CJ wanted change. Here he was in the midst of a roaring crowd who couldn't get enough of the sound they heard. As his violin swooned the audience, his soul was freed. Kids, all kinds, all ages, all nationalities. The different life styles just heightened the music.

There she was in all her differences and leaned against the wall as her holey sneakers keep beat with the base rhythm. Her hair was the color of an autumn forest; her eyes flashed upbringing. She walked and owned the room. Nobody dared look at her. But I did. My eyes met their match. Cool and airy, she didn't care what anyone thought. But before I could look away she sat right down, close as she could get to me. It was hard to concentrate with those eyes examining every bit of me. She didn't smile, didn't move, as if the music froze her.

There was a short break so I took my chances.

"Do you like our music?" I know it was a stupid question but nothing else came to my mind. She just looked at me and nodded. I haven't seen you at school. Do you play an instrument?"

"CJ you are wasting your time."

"It's my time."

"No, you don't get it. Valerie can't hear you. Beautiful as she is, her hands speak for her. If you can't hear them, it's over." A knotted pang hit my stomach. Sickened, I remembered my own vicious self- pity. Valerie had everything but couldn't really enjoy any of it. "Up close, she felt the vibrations of the music. Bet you thought it was you. We all did."

The second set I played my heart out. Valerie tapped, then swayed listening to music no one else could hear. The thought never occurred to me that my ears might not hear. From now on, my thanksgiving would never stop. I no longer cared if the whole world knew that I lived in a tunnel. Before I could even really try to communicate with Valerie, she disappeared. Her presence left a dent in my head. My silent quest possessed me.

MY QUEST

At school, I attacked the library. I was a soldier on my very own mission. Once I found the signing books, Victoria and I practiced with one another. It was tricky in the tunnel with little light but the oil lamp burned with encouragement. Having my mind focused on something other than my feelings quickened my pace. Each letter was formed exactly with the fingers. Never could I imagine that my fingers could make so many shapes. And putting the letters together into words was challenging. If you forgot a letter it was over. Victoria came up with letter drills that helped imprint them in my brain.

With homework and drills, the days flew by. Seeing Victoria happy was so unexpected. Eating a lot of her product, we survived nicely on gooey pretzels. At the stand, Victoria conversed with the best and the worst of them. Customers flocked to see her then remembered the pretzels.

With or without your permission, living in a tunnel changed your perspective. When you had nothing, everything was a possibility. That became my philosophy. At school, I excelled knowing that one way or another Valerie would hear about it.

"CJ have you ever considered the debate team? Your wit would go a long way." Mr. Pen, my English teacher enjoyed my scrunched-up hesitation. "Random topics are chosen and arguments made for or against the stated thesis. It takes thinking on your feet and convincing people. You are a natural. There are competitions between other schools with state and national finals." Suddenly I was interested. "The first practice is today after school. I have submitted your name as a contender. A committee makes the final decision." The day couldn't end quickly enough. Quite a number of kids piled into Mr. Pen's classroom. The expected type: glasses, studious, khakis, white shirts, the no riskers. Nothing about me fit in until I opened up my mouth. Everything that I went through, changed my insight. I was the richest of kids, now the poorest, the coolest of kids, with three or four musical friends, and nothing ever mattered, now everything mattered, before my life faded away day into day, now every day was a totally new adventure. This brought punch to my opinions. The trial topic was how your environment affected you. With no effort at all, I wove together many things that happened to me. Everyone was amazed at my imagination and my perspective. Too bad it was more real than the rain pouring outside. Six kids were chosen and I was one of them. Cool purple and black t-shirts were given to us to be worn at every practice and event. A new clean t-shirt was just what I needed.

With the chosen six, there was a wiry thread of respect among us. Each of us was a mouth piece, different notes but all the same chorus. Words forced me to listen to look inside instead of relying on appearances. It was neat being the youngest but having the most to say.

I couldn't help but overhear one of the girls. "His mind, wonderful, but couldn't wait to get away from him, his clothes. . .ugh." Then and there I needed to figure out how to get rid of the ugh. Eliot put it all in perspective. "Clothes don't make the man but clean clothes help."

A few blocks down from school was a laundry mat where you did your own laundry. Back in my privileged life, my clothes were always sent to the cleaners even my jeans, starched and pressed was a must. The laundry mat was so frustrating because you had to wait, no way to hurry the load. There was also the problem of the detergent. There was an old forgotten cupboard that graciously housed my soap box. While my clothes spun, I studied. I worked on essays for the debate club and practiced my sign language. It all fell into place. My gym locker was the holding tank for my dirty clothes. Then twice a week I hauled it down to the laundry mat, fully prepared to stay busy. What a relief, now the girls drew numbers to determine who would sit next to me or so I imagined.

On day Mr. Pen announced that there was to be a mock trial for the debate club that was opened to other schools. You would have thought that it was How to win the lottery, the word spread like the coolest sneakers just went on sale and only two pairs remained. Everyone was curious to see who the selected few were and if they were the robots of the school. For kids to be that interested in a studious club amazed me.

The big day arrived. Mr. Pen was a proud, colorful peacock whose feathers fluttered in every direction. All dressed up in a brown stripped suit complemented with dark brown tie loafers, he brought dignity to the event. I was a little peacock myself, feathers fully spread. Anything could happen. Kids from different schools poured into the cafeteria which was decorated with banners promoting the debate. Ten teams, two from each school. There were mascots and a sponsor that sat with each team cueing them verbally in one way or another.

Waiting for the topic, I scouted around and considered my opposition. At one of the side tables, there she was in all her mystery, Valerie, signing with her interpreter. My mind stopped and my heart took over. Everything in me wanted to bust out of my chair and run to her. My debate partner noticed I was suddenly unglued.

"CJ now isn't the time for any distractions. Pull yourself together. Remember right now it's not what you do, but what you say that counts."

Mr. Pen cleared his voice and announced the topic, "How adversity strengthens life." Before I knew it, we were race horses, up and running. We were given three minutes to convince and three minutes for rebuttal. Forcing myself to look away from Valerie, I organized my thoughts and my delivery. Everyone spoke clearly and skillfully. When it came to Valerie's team, the interpreter spoke for her. I didn't need to hear a word. I read her hands easily. All my hard work paid off. As she finished, I signed back what a wonderful job she had done. The biggest grin I ever saw flashed across her face. Suddenly nothing else mattered, not what I said or didn't say. The most beautiful face lit up the room. Respect gushed out of me. I lost all sense of where I was and what I did. Valerie's hands were clasped in mine and I never let her go.

It was time for the rebuttal. During the past year, I taught myself how to fight verbally; intelligently. Everyone got very quiet. Even the sponsors zoomed in on what I said. Being a verbal target, I loved every minute of it. At any cost, I was here to impress. Valerie's fingers roared with admiration. Up next, Valerie was equally as gifted with her retort. As if predetermined, it was between her team and ours for the final rebuttal. The two teams were coached by their sponsors. The two mascots paraded around and drummed up cries of support for both teams. It got pep rally loud. On his given signal, Mr. Pensin quieted the group quickly down.

Everyone got ready to win. I already won; Valerie's eyes and mine were locked together for the remaining debate. With her rebuttal on deafness, alienation, and the power to overcome, Valerie's team won. I was the first to congratulate her in her own language.

Funny how when it was all over, then I got very nervous. The drama was over but the intensity just began. Walking over to Valerie's table, I lost my footing and almost tripped on a broken tile. Not even a quick smirk on her part. All I saw was concern. As I sat down, she grasped me with both hands Fingers flew this way and that. We laughed, we understood, we flushed like a red-hot ember. A turning point for me; I could do anything. My inner mission began.

OTHERS

||||||||||||||||||||||||||||||||||||||||||||||||||||||||||||||||||||||||||||||||||||||||||||||||||||||||||||||||||||||||||||||||||||||||

Outside the temperature dropped. The pretzel- stand lost its charm. Victoria's face paled. Lines of renewed adversity were plowed snow banks on either side of her mouth. Inside work was a must.

One day at school, there was a big gap in the cafeteria's serving line. Some of the employees were out with the flu and the food just wasn't being cooked or served quickly enough for anyone. Apologizing, the head cashier quickly explained the situation and just tried to calm the kids and hurried teachers who were anxious to get back their classes. A window of opportunity slid silently open. I could hardly wait to tell Victoria.

Bursting with expectation, Victoria escorted me to school bright and early the next day. The restroom's mirror confirmed her confidence. She could cook and prepare anything, especially healthy food for teenagers. Her vegetable laden Chinese background would be an asset.

Approaching the maze-like cafeteria, Victoria found herself toe to toe with the manager.

"Miss this is off bounds for you. You have to have permission to be back here. It's a bonded area only for food preparation, food professionals if you will. You need a food badge."

"I have a food badge, just forgot to wear it. Food preparation is second nature to me. There will be no waiting bins in this cafeteria line. My son is a student here and thought you might need some help."

With that said, Victoria was led into the kitchen, given plastic gloves, a uniform and prepared food The warmth of the double oven rekindled every muscle in her body. An energized glow poured through her. Never again would she stand on that street corner with winter's breath hounding her. She almost forgot what it was like to be in a real kitchen with electric lights, opening cupboards, solid counters and real refrigerators that opened and closed.

A few hours later, kids poured in like running water.

"Could I have another helping please?" Victoria knew that voice; she loved that voice. Her son melted as she heaped potatoes and gravy on his plate. She was so thankful that she slipped a few extra dollars in his pocket this morning. From now on, things would be very different. Pretzels were off the menu.

Victoria was warm, uniformed, and fit right in with the rest of them. With her hair pinned back, I forgot how beautiful she was. Imagine starting every day together in the same place other than a tunnel.

"Hey CJ did you check out the new babe dishing out potatoes?"

"That babe is my mother."

"Oh sorry she is just so pretty; younger, that's what I meant to say." Part of me wanted to punch him and the other part of me agreed with him. The school buzzed. Older kids slapped me on the back and commented on my genetic makeup. Most of the girls cared less. What a relief that now during the day Victoria and I were both warm and ate food that was actually good for us.

Uncontained, Eric bounded over. "CJ you have just got to go with me. Every year we put on a school play. One of the leads dared me to go with him on an audition. Something about acting, playing a part. Hey we are musicians. We kind of act on the stage, not exactly but I figured it was worth a try. Are you in? Oh yeah, some prepping is involved. You know it's all about the looks. Clean, hair just right, girly stuff. Come with me after school today, and my mom will put the finishing touches on our hair. A hair dresser for years, she could style your hair blindfolded."

Until at least five-thirty, Victoria prepped food for the next day. The outside no longer dictated our every move.

Not too far from school, Eric, his sisters, and mother lived in a cramped apartment. His dad never showed up to be counted. Not seen or heard, he was sorely missed. Eric filled in the widening gap. When his sisters jabbered, I found out way more than I wanted to know. Some things were better left blank.

"CJ, how about some tuffs in the back and on the sides?" queried Martha. It was almost a year since I cut my hair. Before I started school, I chopped some of it off but not very well. At school, they measured the length. No exceptions, either it was or it wasn't. If it wasn't, you fixed it or spent the year in home schooling.

"Hair to me is like music to the two of you; it frees me, allows me to create something beautiful." And with that said, I laid back in the swivel chair and my mind let go. Martha turned me this way and that. She had quite a time loosening the pink goop out of my hair and cut out matted bits. Martha knew neglect when she saw it.

"CJ, don't use the pink soap any more. It will damage your hair. Your hair needed some tender loving care. A good feathered pillow might help." A feathered pillow? How about a dirt floor, some fake grass, and a torn-up blanket? I almost asked her. But I didn't want to make a scene. Slowly, I began to feel like a person again, oddly human, that people even cared what happened to me. Without warning, my flood gates broke. Everything was held in for so long. Heaving, I just collapsed.

Martha was eerily quiet and urged her words, "Whatever it is CJ, it will eventually work out. I promise you. One day at a time that's the only rule around here, should be everywhere."

"That's a good rule. Where we live there are no rules." And so I told Martha everything. Her eyes got so big and almost burst out of her head.

"From now on, our home is your home. Whatever you need, let Eric know and he will be more than happy to share with you." With my spirit, I clung to Martha's words. Martha ached for CJ and Victoria. She was unaware that tunnels were a home for any kid. Someone intervened for her. It was time to give back. She stuffed CJ's backpack full of ready to eat packaged foods and a bottle of shampoo. It was a small step but still a step.

Victoria couldn't believe her eyes. Her handsome son returned. His good looks didn't wait to be acknowledged; they jumped out at her. Her sheer joy shouted back.

"Victoria, just a little rearranging that's all. Real shampoo, a trained hair dresser, and of course all my hair was washed at the same time. Remember how we used to do that?" Victoria chuckled. Though they had nothing, they had everything. Victoria was so grateful that she had an opportunity to really get to know her son, inside and out before CJ really became a man.

But already a young confident man gazed back at her. A pied piper at school, CJ was a kid magnet yet attracted teachers as well. Victoria remembered long ago when CJ fainted in the grocery store if his teachers talked to him. Those days were gone.

Interrupting and red in the face, Samuel burst in.

"CJ, you don't have much time. They will make it so you can't leave. Don't leave any of your stuff behind. During the day, you have become too noticeable. People are asking more and more questions. There are too few answers. You haven't given back. Working people don't live in tunnels. Everything in me wanted to stay and fight, but then I remembered there were two of us. Victoria was beyond vulnerable.

It was still early in the evening. Instinctively, Victoria grabbed her uniform, a quilt and her other pair of jeans. I yanked my violin case out of the brush and noticed the lock was scratched up. Low voices from way down the hall got closer. With no time to spare, Samuel and I shoved up the tunnel's lid.

"Samuel, I want you to know that I will not forget about you or the other kids. One way or another I will help you. Tell them." And with that said, Victoria urged me up as I felt cold, thin, spindly fingers grab my leg. With all my might, I kicked and heard someone moan. I slammed the lid down as hard as I could and put a loaded trash can on top of it. It would give us time to blend into the shapeless mases.

NEW YORK'S NIGHT

New York's night was way different than the day. It was a grownup's universe. Kids were not welcome, not allowed. Women with gobs of makeup and short skirts were everywhere., so different than the girls at school. Victoria just told me they were street people, trying to make ends meet. We were all pretty much the same, yesterday's leftovers.

Victoria was used to the tunnel's warmth and whatever false security it provided. She and CJ were now the night's prey. Victoria remembered the spewing sewer vent, gulping and spitting out much needed heat. But the old vent was completely roped off and abandoned, no plastic tents, not a trace of anyone ever being there. Makeshift cardboard boxes were only a botched memory. There had to be another way. The restrooms were already jammed with families and young kids In my mind, a flash light burst.

"Victoria the laundry mat is still open."

"What laundry mat?" CJ then remembered he never actually took her there. CJ felt her exhaustion. Victoria's first day at work took its toll. He would get her needed heat and the food in his back pack would give them much needed energy. His relentless chant was 'Just get to the laundry mat.'

It was warm and nearly empty. Pulling two chairs over in a corner, Victoria and I waited for laundry that wasn't there. After an hour, Mrs. Pit the owner recognized me and wandered over.

"CJ this is not your normal routine."

"My mother and I were just evicted and just need a warm place for a few more hours. "

"Well you can't sleep very well in a chair. Would a couple of cots and a heater make a difference? There is a spare room in back that needs visitors. It has been complacent for much too long." Though not really my type, I could have kissed Mrs. Pit. Victoria jumped up and hugged Mrs. Pit. "I have a job at the school, I will pay good money for this room."

"Let's just get you settled and out of this drafty air." Mrs. Pit was very fond of CJ and would have done anything to help him. There was just something so different about him. Different kids mattered; they changed things. And his hard-working mother confirmed her thoughts. Being alone and without wasn't easy. Years ago, quite un-expectantly, Mr. Pit contracted a deadly virus. One day he was here and the next he wasn't. The laundry mat was her way of giving back, making laundry more pleasant. A plate of cookies was always within reach and she made a point to know everyone by name. The kids who visited claimed her heart since her only son enlisted in the army and never returned. Both the men in her life left her without so much as a goodbye.

The spare room wasn't used to visitors. Dust was everywhere and cobwebs drifted between corners. But the warmth in that little room radiated throughout and warmed every cold, anxious thought. The cots were barely used, if ever. Mrs. Pit warmed up some meatloaf and greens from her dinner and brought them back to us. She lived in an attachment to the building. A twinkle in Mrs. Pit's eye never went out. That twinkle of hope and goodness kept us alive that night; I was certain of it.

A few hours later, a scraping sound woke me up from a drifting dream. Rustling and clinging of coins was heard from the laundry room. Then a detestable voice rang out, "Let's just see what's in the next room." There was no time to wake up Victoria so I crouched behind a closet door. "Well who do we have here; if it isn't Miss too good for others." Victoria moaned as a boot kicked the bed. "We should have done this a long time ago." With only seconds to spare I kicked as hard as I could where kicks are unaccustomed to going. Instantly, his knees knelt to the ground.

"It's the kid; let's get him." The two druggies came at me and with just a few punches fell into one another's arms. Victoria staggered up and easily tied their slimy hands together with bed sheets.

One direct kick was hardly enough. When I turned around the tunnel master was on me like a disease.

"It's better this way kid. It has always been between you and me. Just waited for the right time." With hatred and contempt, the tunnel master's yellowish eyes glowed in the dark. His claws were out and ready to rip.

Everything in me said run, but I stood and faced him. Being the protective mother that she was, Victoria screamed at the top of her blood curdling lungs. The tunnel master laughed eerily.

"Now who do you suppose will hear you? It's four o'clock in the morning. Much too early for doing laundry wouldn't you say?" No sooner had he said that, a four o'clock voice answered him.

"Get away from the kid or I will blow your head off." There was Mrs. Pit in all her glory holding a pistol with steady hands.

"Lady do you really think that will stop any of this?" Before you could blink, the pistol went off whizzing by his glowing eyes.

"The four o'clock voice commanded, "CJ listen to me closely. There are cuffs in my robe. They might be a little rusty but they will do. Mr. Pit always thought they might come in handy one day." Being a retired policeman had its benefits. This was better than any script for any audition. Jamming those cuffs on the tunnel master was a defining moment of my life.

Victoria was spell bound as she watched CJ yank the defeated tattoos together that hung limply on the master's bony hands. But that was just the beginning of the show. Lights and sirens were everywhere screaming louder than Victoria could ever cry. It must have been an early fourth of July. The whole laundry mat was lit up in expectation. Loud megaphones blared warnings that were unneeded. The intruders were already down. The druggies had passed out and the tunnel master was sprawled in a corner cursing the interference with choice words.

Looking around Pete, the head officer, gave Mrs. Pit a sheepish grin. "Not much more needs to be done around here. Your husband always said you could take care of yourself and anyone else. He was right about that little lady." Mrs. Pit felt pride's rush; her husband was still remembered after all of these years. Tears of relief sprung out of her. Her husband knew what she didn't. Warning someone with a bullet was one thing, hitting someone was quite another. Before the officers arrived, red on a matador's coat reeled through Mrs. Pit's mind. As the red faded into blue, her mind whirled into stillness. Pete commanded, "Let's get this trash out of here so these people can get back to sleep."

Being the little lady that she was Mrs. Pit insisted the officers have some of her warmed banana bread. Wafts of banana bread intoxicated the air. The intruders were hauled off. All in all, it was a night's gala that I would never forget.

THE AUDITION

Early the next morning, Mrs. Pit insisted on hot steamy showers. The water pressure invigorated every nerve in my body. It was different than the locker room set-up. Mrs. Pit's shower had the girly stuff, sweet smelling soap, berry shampoo, all kinds of sea sponges and different sized towels monogramed with her initials. Most of me refused to leave that bathroom. Mrs. Pit must have read my mind.

"CJ you can use this bathroom any time." Again, I could have kissed her. Loaded up with pancakes, homemade syrup, and greasy dripping bacon, I was ready for the audition. Before I left, Mrs. Pit suggested that I wear one of her son's shirts that was crisply pressed and still hung on a hanger after fifteen years. Still in style, I was really thankful that I wore something different. Smelling like berries and looking like a kid with taste, I headed for school. Every nerve in me twitched as I paced myself throughout the day. Eric's mind probably worked like mine.

He looked like he couldn't wait for the last bell. Earlier, Eric's mom puffed up his hair and surprised him with some new cologne since he had a tendency to overheat. When the closing bell rang, Eric spied CJ down the hall surrounded with girls. They couldn't miss their ride. Urgency hurried the boys to the prearranged pick-up area but no one was there.

"They just left. You really didn't think the jocs would wait for you, did you?" A gawky kid commented as he watched our faces fall. "But not to worry, Mr. Sears is one of the judges and hasn't left yet." Who was this kid? The geek who knew everything about everybody? "He's right over there if you are going to ask him for a ride." Neither of us knew Mr. Sears but that didn't stop us. A ride was a ride. Who drove didn't really matter.

With some hesitation, we were squished into Mr. Sear's back seat with all of his boxes and papers. A marked teacher, he didn't need to say a word. But within minutes he spoke. "Boys I can only take you part way. It's a rule that no one can collaborate with the judges. But I will get you within a block or so."

So much for the primping. By the time we got to the right building, we were a mess. Eric had the good sense to take a detour and get our looks back under control. Good looking kids were everywhere. The local schools must have released all of their star quarter backs. Then and there, I decided that it was about Eric's audition and not mine.

The door revolved constantly. As soon as one kid went in, one kid came out. Heads shook one way than another. Eric couldn't sit still. He rounded the room again and again. His thoughts filled the room. Getting this audition would change his life completely. No matter what it took he would snatch it out of any body's hand. Hours passed. Most everyone left.

Finally, Eric's name was called. Determined, he marched in and faced some drawn faces.

"Son, I know this isn't easy. We would like for you to read this dialogue as a dejected, homeless boy." The total opposite of Eric who was the provider for his family; looked upon as the father and he read it as such. Just as he finished one page, one of the tired faces stopped him and thanked him for his time. "Hey kid, is there anyone else out there?" Eric's longing for the part shut down as quickly as it had jump started.

"There is another kid out there. I will tell him." Eric knew no handsome football player would get this part, no quirky musician, but a homeless kid who knew the streets. It was a privilege to know that kid.

Before I knew it, Eric insisted and pushed me through the door. I sat down before the panel and looked around the room. My eyes darted in and out, taking a picture of the room, looking for another way out in case I needed it. It was a habit of mine that never went away. "Tell us about yourself," suggested Mr. Andros one of the interested voices.

"There isn't much to tell. I'm certain you have listened to plenty all afternoon."

"That's where you're wrong. So what about you? Do we make you nervous?"

"No, not at all. I wasn't even sure if I would make it through the night. Every breath that I take isn't a given. When you have nothing, you have nothing to lose. Up until last night, we lived in the tunnels."

"You mean the subways?"

"No, the underground tunnels. We were evicted because my mother found a job but didn't share the profits. Drug addicts, abusers, and lost children were our companions. Does that make you nervous?"

"Yes. Would you please read this?" As I started to read, I knew that I couldn't finish it. The words were too vivid, too real. Half-way through my voice choked and I put the paper down.

"Sorry. This isn't for me. It's not a part. It's my life." As I looked up, the three drawn faces were ash white, and humbled.

"You're just who we searched for. This audition was about your life, that's the part."

"You mean you want somebody like me?'

"No, we want you." I was pretty sure there was a misunderstanding but then a bunch of papers fluttered everywhere. "Your mother needs to come in and okay all of this. You do have that mother you talked about, don't you? You see CJ this is for a movie, a real movie and we need your mother's permission." I was dumbfounded. "And that's not all. You will earn a substantial amount of money for this part. You and your mother will be well provided for and not have to worry about living in another tunnel as long as you live." My heart jumped roped. "CJ do you want this part?"

"Well I'm school, have homework, laundry and am a part time musician."

"Even better, we'll work around your schedule. Whatever we need to do we will do. You need to get ready to be spoiled. You will have a car at your disposal to pick you up at school, meals will be provided for you and your mother, and an apartment of your choice will be rented for you. How does that sound?"

That expression when your ears burn, well my ears were on fire. At any minute I was sure they would tell me it was just a joke, a really well played out joke. Maybe just to see how kids reacted to everything they ever dreamed of. Well I decided to put it to the test.

"Would it be alright for my friends to come in on the set and watch what I do?" Their faces didn't change a bit.

"As long as they're quiet, why not? CJ we would really like you to say yes to this. But it is your decision." It got really quiet. "Would home schooling make the deal? We would provide a teacher for you so you wouldn't have to go to school. That way your day would be freed so that you could be here early in the morning to shoot the movie. Does that sound good to you?" Not to have to go to school every day and listen to the up and coming comments would be just about perfect. "it's okay CJ to get a little excited."

Somehow thank you didn't seem to be enough. "It's just all so surreal. Something that you would really want so that you could help others who so badly need help. It's just been so hard for so long. And I have met so many others worse off than myself. It would be a way to make things right. Yes, I would really like to do it."

"Well than that settles it. CJ you sound like you are twenty but I know that you aren't. How old are you? I am well in my teens."

"But not eighteen, are you?"

"Well no. I'm in ninth grade." I must have said something really funny because they all laughed like they would burst. Before my very eyes, their faces changed. Kindness erupted.

"Let's get your mom in here right away so we can celebrate." That afternoon Eric and Victoria both wept for different reasons. Eric, because he already knew that the part was mine and Victoria because I was her son. A hurricane of pride swept through her.

Right away, everything changed. We were ushered into a high-end clothing store to get enough outfits for at least a month. Victoria blended right in with the other ladies. Her makeup was on perfectly and Mrs. Pit did her hair in one of those swirly, curly styles. Actually Mrs. Pit didn't let us out of her sight but insisted on going with us. I mean who would have believed any of it? The three of us were transformed together. Delighted, Mrs. Pit was overwhelmed since the stylish clothing was nothing that a policeman's wife would ever think of wearing. Victoria smiled uneasily. Time had changed her. Clothes no longer identified her. Choosing clothes, I was a kid again. Not like before because now I knew what it was like not to have any. Credit cards were bags of chips that were passed out and devoured. This new world seemed limitless. But I reminded myself that we were only visiting.

Shopping made you hungry. Sparcos, the best restaurant in town, awaited. Apparently, we had a reservation, and were seated immediately. There were others who tried to talk their way in but were turned away. Dressed in our best there was no distinction between the other customers and ourselves. Starched white linen table cloths draped the table and crystal glasses clanged when you hit them with a fork. Nothing new, I saw it all before a very long time ago. But names from the menu that I couldn't even pronounce got my attention. Mother and Mrs. Pitzin also looked puzzled. Taking command, Mr. Andros ordered for all of us.

Before you could say celebration, a chilled bottle of champagne arrived. When popped open, all that I enjoyed was the scented spray. Everyone enjoyed Victoria who made quite an impression on the other guests. Once she remembered, her manners were impeccable. Mrs. Pit was hypnotized as Victoria cracked the lobster and broke off its claws scooping out the rich buttery meat.

The best was saved for last. Our flaming dessert was tossed with fruit brandy and vanilla ice cream as huge bing-cherries perched on top of the sweetness. In between cherries, Mr. Andros tossed back his tie and carefully unfolded the designated contract. After it was read out loud, a golden encrusted pen appeared out of nowhere.

"it's an Italian pen; the one we always use." Dancing figures covered it. Just holding the pen was exciting. It twirled effortlessly in my hand. Scribbling my signature like a doctor surprised Mr. Andros. "Quite a signature for a ninth grader," chuckled Mr. Andros who enjoyed the moment thoroughly.

Thoughts swirled around the table. Mrs. Pitzin was so grateful to CJ for possibility that opened up. Mr. Andros admired Victoria as much as the lad. A part for her might very well appear in his own life. Being single suddenly paled. CJ stumbled into manhood knowing he could now finally fulfill his father's parting words to take care of his mother. Four lives were forever changed with a stroke of an Italian pen.

LIFE ON ANOTHER SIDE

onfirming that it really happened, Victoria and I danced excitedly around the room. Last night as we said our adieus, Mr. Andros drove up to this swanky apartment, handed us the keys, and announced that the apartment's years lease was paid in full. Simultaneously, our three jaws dropped. Mrs. Pitzin was tempted to board up her laundry mat and move in.

The refrigerator was stocked full of healthy food that waited to be enjoyed. There was a wine-rack bursting with Victoria's favorite wine. Elegant curtains with sheer under garments hung effortlessly from the windows. The furniture even matched the curtains. How could any man know just what to do? If you ask me, Mr. Andros knew way too much and held Victoria's hand way too long last night. But she didn't complain; never said a word.

Even the bathroom was another world. A jutted tub with sky lights was surrounded by heated floor tiles. The water got hot quickly and stayed hot. There was enough hot water for three baths if you needed them. Burying myself in a thick terry towel, I realized it was softer than the sheets.

But today was more exciting than any of that. With school closed down for vacation, Victoria also had some days off. What better way to spend it than on a movie set watching me perform as myself? The car was scheduled to pick us up in an hour. For sure, the kids from school already heard who got the sought-after part. Eric didn't need a telephone; he was one. I wondered if she knew? I wouldn't have long to wait.

In the run-down south side of town, an old abandoned building was turned into a movie set. Deserted apartment buildings were on the right and an old boarded up, fallen down school was on the left. Here, you expected to find homeless children. Glamorous described none of it. The actual set was completely roped off. Other actors milled around not at all interested in anything but themselves. Mr. Andros couldn't wait until we arrived.

Victoria spied him first. Mr. Andros' nick name was checker. It fit him perfectly as he examined every little detail. Ultimately, it was his responsibility to persuade our eyes to believe what we saw.

"CJ is there anything on the set that you would change?" There were some things that didn't fit. The outdoor setting was all wrong, much too refined. There needed to be broken, decayed, withered stuff. Broken tree limbs, ripped clothing, and cardboard boxes. That's what it lacked.

"To be authentic there needs to be signs of struggle, brokenness, and shreds of discarded life. Just walk along the streets and don't stumble among the cardboard boxes, where the homeless hide."

"The kid's right. Mess this set up a little." On the set, Mr. Andros was a different man, totally absorbed, involved in every decision. Victoria was drawn to that part of him, that control thing. That he knew where everybody was and what they needed to do.

After some primping, we were ready to go. Victoria had a labeled chair right next to Mr. Andros. I drifted in and out as I got accustomed to the mismatched clothes and went over my dialogue. Almost hearing my name, I turned around and there she was, her eyes on fire and her fingers flying through a workout. Valerie was all dressed up and shone like a red garnet. Red was everywhere in her hair, outfit, and lips, big bright bold red lipstick that wouldn't be missed.

"I wore red so you would see me," her silent words spoke. Valerie was so beautiful I would have kissed her right then and there if Victoria hadn't interrupted.

"CJ who is your friend?" I was that proud peacock at the park with its feathers spread for all to see.

"Mother, Mr. Andros this is Valerie, my friend from school."

"Well, I didn't think that you met her in the tunnel," chuckled Mr. Andros. It was supposed to be funny but wasn't. No one said a word but Valerie thought he was lame among other choice words. You could tell that Mr. Andros had never lacked a single day in his privileged life. He had a lot to learn; I would be the one to teach him.

Our intense signing lessons paid off. Fingers to fingers, Victoria talked with Valerie as the set grew very quiet. Other actors were in the "zone" as they called it. Getting myself into the part wasn't necessary; it was my life. Mr. Andros didn't influence me one way or the other. It was going to be my part, my way, and it was. Some of my dialogue was so stiff, so unnatural that I just adlibbed and added my own words. Mr. Andros interrupted everyone else but never said a word to me. Every time I spoke his eyes filmed over, distant as if somewhere else. Then darting in and out, he jumped up from his chair and redirected the actors. The opening episode was electric, a 100watt light show. It was all sensory: seeing it, tasting it, hearing it, feeling it. My spontaneity inspired the other actors and pretty soon there was no script.

Victoria did her best to distract Mr. Andros but without success. Most men used to fall at her feet, but her feet changed and were no longer innocent. Valerie was also very pre-occupied. Her eyes documented everything as she sketched some of the scenes zooming in on CJ and his reactions.

Jittery, Mr. Andros jumped up and announced lunch. Before you knew it, fancy ham and cheese finger sandwiches were brought in with glazed strawberry molded salads and ice cream desserts.

"CJ, I have a surprise for you. I changed things up a bit and added the tunnel to the movie. It's in the next take. Thought you would be pleased." It was all a bit too real. But what was a tunnel without the kids? My question was answered before I asked it.

Eric's input reached further than I imagined. As if on cue, Eric, a piped piper, walked in with a bunch of the tunnel kids following.

"Thought you might want some company; the kids couldn't wait to see you." Starving fingers finished off the left-over sandwiches and everything else that was in sight. As if in a trance, Mr. Andros stared at the new comers. They would be extras in the next scene. The kids didn't need any primping; they were naturally messed up. Their clothes were perfect. Excited, they were placed along the sides of the tunnel's walls. The scene was overwhelming, so dramatic that the electricity burst. Knowing that it was the kid's reality, Mr. Andros became a wilted rose just pulled up from a lovely, well- watered garden.

The afternoon was a blue winged heron that flew by. The neglected kids approached Mr. Andros. The ringleader spoke. "Mister, we just want to thank you for the best afternoon that we ever had. We ate, we laughed, we were allowed to have some fun. Being a kid shouldn't always be such a struggle. Today was little bit of heaven." Something had to give; these kids deserved a life any kind of a life outside of a tunnel. He remembered a co-worker who adopted kids, pedigree kids who came from good families but just didn't fit in. These kids were never given any chance so who knew what remained locked inside them. He agonized.

CJ blossomed and bloomed. Valerie couldn't take her eyes off of him. If nothing else, this opportunity had given him everything he ever wanted, a chance to be cherished again by someone his own age. A malt shop was a few blocks away and CJ and Valerie slipped out without anyone noticing. It was the first time alone together without onlookers. Just the two of them sipping goopy, chocolate milk shakes without a care in the world. Fingers were so much quieter than words. It gave you time to say exactly what you wanted to say. So the wrong thoughts never had a chance to come out.

Her fingers slowed way down. "I just thought you were like all the rest of the musicians just wanting to be seen with me. But that isn't you. It's so wonderful to find someone I can really talk to and have them really understand. My parents have done so much for me but now it's up to me. Kind of like you and your mom. That it's your turn to grab on to life and make it what you will." Unable to stop them, my tears melted into my ice cream. The last kind words that were spoken to me was so long ago. Valerie's words hurt my ears in a powerful way.

Funny, we weren't missed at all. Mr. Andros surprised Victoria with a huge bouquet of lavender, pink, and golden flowers and a bottle of champagne. He knew women. Way off in the corner, there was an iridescent light that glittered around both of them. For once, I was invisible to my mother. It was a good feeling in a way knowing someone else could make her this happy. Maybe Mr. Andros had more to him than I thought; mother was a good judge of character.

Today showed me who I was and who I wasn't. I thought it was going to be all about the movie. But it was all about what went on around the movie. None of it was about me. It was all about the others that made the difference. Seeing the kids again yanked every heart strings apart. Those kids were not going to remain discarded. Now I had the means and the way to make it right.

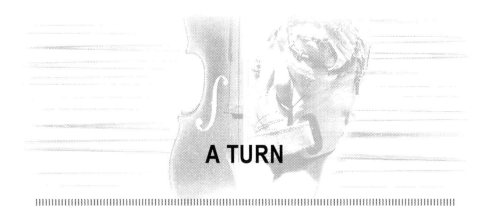

A TURN

For days in a row, the tunnel kids came back, were fed, laughed, and had a chance to be kids. But knowing where they retreated to after dark haunted me. The streets taught me what mattered and what didn't. When life wronged you, it was about doing what was right. One afternoon, this burning desire erupted.

Ugly black and blue bruises covered Sam's arms. He huddled in a corner and wouldn't say a word. The other kids were very quiet and everyday grins were overcast, gloomy, stormy. The wind of change swept silently into the set.

"Sam, whatever happened to you?"

"He got out of jail, the tunnel master, on a technicality and regained his turf with a vengeance. At arm's length, I was the raw dough that he beat over and over. He tried to choke the very life out of me. All because I wouldn't eat his food. I wasn't at all hungry because of all the wonderful fresh food that we eat here. Dumpster food has a smell and flavor all of its own. I can't go back there. I thought he liked me."

"You don't have to. You are coming home with me. All are and that settles it." The rest of the kids started crying. One by one, the boys uncovered unsightly cuts and recent gashes from bits of glass that the druggies marked them with.

"They told me I had to be marked to stay in the tunnel. It hurt so bad and I hate how it looks. It's all infected and I can't make it well. I rubbed some ice on it to take away the pain but it hurts." I was a double oven with an oozing overdone blueberry pie. Furry bubbled over inside me.

That afternoon we didn't go straight home but instead went to the clinic. One by one the kids were examined and treated for infections and given tetanus shots. Mr. Andros came up with some kind of plausible explanation, a camping trip that went horribly wrong. The doctors just shook their heads in disbelief. Never witnessing abuse, Mr. Andros got violently ill and the doctors gave him a shot as well.

Once the tears stopped and stomachs quieted, things changed. I never imagined that all the kids would be able to fit in the apartment but they did. The floor was covered with soft air mattresses, sheets and blankets, transformed into a makeshift dorm. Each kid spent a lifetime in the bathroom and was given clean clothes. Mr. Andros surprised us all with a home cooked meal, more than enough to be a Thanksgiving dinner. Victoria's trained hands jumped right in as sauces and assorted meats were in every pot then comingled together in a giant oven pan. No one went without that night. Refusing to leave, Mr. Andros muttered something about not wanting to miss anything. His heart opened up to kids who never knew a man who didn't hurt them.

In the middle of the night, a whimpering cry disarmed me. Drenched with sweat, Sam woke up. "He's after me; he's after me. He's going to kill me." Grabbing Sam, I shook him back to his senses. But I couldn't stop the fear. Instinctively, Mr. Andros pulled Sam up and held him to his chest. "Now you listen here Sammy, no one is going to hurt you. They will have to get through me to get to you." That did it. Sam's little puffed up face relaxed and a huge sigh escaped from his throbbing chest. There was an epidemic of tears. One by one, Mr. Andros held each child and love whispered it was a night that I will never forget. Sleep was a thief that carried us away.

Saturday broke through. It was a slumber party that never stopped. Story after story. Scrawny Joe couldn't wait to tell us what happened to him. "I was so hungry and came back empty handed with no swiped stuff. You couldn't eat without giving something. I smelled, saw, and touched food all around me but wasn't allowed to eat it. The more I cried, the more they laughed. I tried to get out of the tunnel, but they just shoved me backwards. I told them I would rather die then live another moment and he handed me a syringe full of liquid stuff and urged me to do it. I spit in his face, and hid way back in the tunnel in the dirt."

Mr. Andros changed the taunting tide of abuse. "Boys we'll have plenty of fun so you'll have nothing but good memories." The skateboard park did the trick. Every boy's dream was to stay on top of a surfboard as it sliced through the waves. This was close enough as we pounced down a thawing skateboard ramp on a teetering skateboard. Fitted with helmets, knee pads, and raw courage, one by one we took the dare. Instead of polarizing fear there was urging joy as each one sought greatness. Some of the kids had no self- confidence whatsoever. Mr. Andros suited up. Down he went. Victoria winced knowing a middle-aged body was not anywhere as agile as a teenager. But what Victoria didn't know that it was all part of Mr. Andros' plan, striving to be the focus of her utmost attention. Maybe it worked a little too well. Hitting the curve, the skateboard flipped from under Mr. Andros and he took some air. Landing, his legs and arms pointed in the wrong direction. Victoria carefully redirected them.

The kids hollered and roared thinking the show was just for them. One by one, they mounted the ramp and challenged it. Voices of newly hatched victory sliced through the air. "I never knew I had it in me." "I actually did it." "If I can do this, I can do anything." A surge of boyhood confidence rose way above any human ugliness. Despite his calamity, Mr. Andros was their biggest cheerleader. A cloud of closeness descended upon us. We became that family that many never had or fate removed.

Part of me just couldn't relate. What about tomorrow, the next day, and the day after? Mr. Andros had a movie to make, and these kids needed more than just one afternoon of joy. Maybe we did more harm than good. They had tasted love, joy, good times. Would it ever be theirs for the taking?

Answers collided with my doubt.

UNACCUSTOMED LOVE

D ays crawled by and were enjoyed by all. Late afternoons burst with fullness. My advanced pay was enough to look for a permanent solution. There was a furnished loft not far from the apartment. It was kid friendly and for rent. Valerie and I investigated.

"Yes, the loft was available but someone over eighteen had to sign for it." The money didn't seem to matter; it was all about the age. Victoria didn't want to be responsible for the wayward kids; she couldn't imagine being in two places at once. The younger boys needed plenty of supervision since they never lived in a family setting. Parents, the one thing that I couldn't provide.

Somehow, Mr. Andros overheard my anguish. "It's the kids right? You know ever since the first night I realized that they were already a family. Each one shared the terror but also trusted in one another. Needing each other was critical; they couldn't be separated. For days, that one single thought dug at me. One by one, foster care would destroy them. They saw, heard, and experienced more than most adults do in a lifetime. Emotional problems alone would send any family into an irreversible tailspin.

They needed a place where they could roam and learn again what it was like to be a kid. For me it was the whole experience: Building forts, camping, watching the sunset and the sunrise in the same day., gathering eggs and feeding animals. Growing up on a farm was probably the only reason I survived. An only child, my pets were my family since my parents worked every minute of every day. There was no dreaming time. I guess that's the reason I was interested in making movies. On a movie set, whatever you imagined became real. Are you up for a ride?"

I was certain that I knew who Mr. Andros was, but I was completely wrong. Without women around, Mr. Andros was a different guy, maybe even a little fun. The surrounding land changed: no more buildings and no more massive sidewalks. The immense sky hugged the land. Blues, purples, reds, and oranges reflected on the melted snow, fallen trees and grasses. Tottering iced fences with broken down barbed wire poked through the fallen debris. Spring was determined to be seen. Blue jays flitted back and forth looking for forgotten nests to raid. In the distance, a slanted, orange rusty colored roof commanded the horizon. It was some kind of a huge barn with numerous stalls. There was no trace of life, not even an abandoned stray cat. A fenced in circular ring begged for wear. Everything waited for something to start.

"CJ, don't let the emptiness fool you. There's a lot here that doesn't meet the eye. What do you see?"

"A rejected place that needs a lot of attention."

"Kind of like those kids, right? Do you think the two would work well together?"

"Like kind of fix each other up? I know when I worked in the restaurant it fixed me up and I started to care again about others. So that's kind of what you said?"

"Yes, that's why the loft wouldn't work. It's too nice, too neat, no brokenness. But out here, troubled hands and minds flourish. Putting something back together again heals. Gets your attention on something else beside you. For example, the movie gave you hope, the chance to provide for your mom. And of course, you met me."

A big grin exploded on his face.

Holding up a discarded bridle Mr. Andros exclaimed. "Well who do you suppose owned this?"

"Some old farmer who can't run with the horses anymore."

"That's exactly right and that's where you and the other kids come in."

"Mr. Andros you mean you're that farmer?"

"Yup, bought it yesterday. Papers signed and sealed. So do you think we can turn this old place around and make a go of it? CJ life can be good. It's not always about the bad stuff. You make your life; your life doesn't make you." While he spoke, Mr. Andros glowed. Rounding the corner, we came up to a bend in the road. There nestled in the trees was the most beautiful farm house I ever saw. It wasn't anything like the rest of the property. Freshly painted red and white paint saturated the walls and chimneys. Windows were everywhere. The sunlight danced its own ballet. It shouted welcome from any side, any angle. The red-faced bricks were sturdy, sunbaked and ready for windy wind, stormy storms and young people.

"CJ, man to man. Do you think that Victoria would enjoy a place like this?"

"You know five minutes ago I would have laughed at you. But this farm house belonged on a post card. It just needed care. Victoria would know just what to do, how to make it smile again."

"Yes, and that's exactly what I want, to make Vitoria smile. My old life was an old pair of blue jeans, no zest, tired and forgotten. Being around movies and actors all the time can make you forget who you really are and who you aren't." Mr. Andros kicked the thawed dirt and hesitated.

"Victoria affects people. You can't just be around her. She gets in the way of things. You want to be around her. Is that what you needed to say?"

"Yes, that pretty much sums it up. But CJ I also want to be around you. Make up for what you haven't had and be someone you can count on."

"But you "do that now. You mean be more than a visitor, more like a china plate rather than a paper plate.

"Yes, that's a good way to put it. Here, I want to show you something. Mr. Andros reached in his pocket and fumbled trying to open the velvet box. It was glittery, sparkled, and would change everything. Will you help me ask her? I mean is it alright with you if I ask her? Right before my very eyes Mr. Andros turned into a seventh-grade kid. An excitement rose up in him that couldn't be contained. He picked me up and twirled me around until we both collapsed laughing hysterically on the ground. Joy answered.

IN THE DISTANCE

|||||||||||||||||||||||||||||||||||||||||||||||||||||||||||||||||||||||||||||||||||||||||||||||||||||||||||||||||||||||||||||||||||||||||||||||||||||||||||||||||||

A soft, persistent voice called out to me through the layers. As if in a kitchen blender, the voice was jumbled-up with spurts, sounds, and words. My ears were unaccustomed to that sound as it strained my ears. It hurt to listen. So far away. But something made me listen. The more I heard, the closer it got. Loving fingers caressed my hair and arms. I knew those fingers.

"His eyelids flickered; he flinched. Keep it up whatever you're doing." There were other background voices. But this one voice insisted.

"CJ you must wake up. You have slept for a very long time. I can't go on without you. Your father and I are both here. You have missed so much school. Your baseball coaches still hold an opening for you on the team. You can't be replaced Your orchestra leader needs your violin's passion. Everyone is praying for you but only you can wake yourself up." What in the world? It sounded like my mother but she was busy at work, or decorating the apartment, or fantasizing about Mr. Andros. And my father was no longer as he remained curled up in a ball in a nursing home. Baseball, I gave my mitt away a long time ago to one of the tunnel kids. My violin knew me casually. I refused to listen and pushed it away. Imposters. Lies. It grew quiet then started up again.

The doctor hesitated. "You have to keep at it. It's the only way. It's almost been too long now. The brain has been inactive for many months. Pretty soon it will choose never to come back."

Her long over defined fingers clutched a beautiful bouquet of fragrant wild flowers that illuminated the auburn redness of her hair. She couldn't get them on the bedside stand quickly enough. Valerie heard that CJ flinched and just had to see it. In love with him, every facet of CJ's face was imprinted on her brain. In her free time when no one else was around, she sketched him for hours.

Most of Valerie's job was to make sure the patients had everything they needed, magazines, ice water, pillows, and menu choices. Valerie felt a kinship with CJ, both of them survived in a silent world. Neither one seemed to have any say about it. But for six months, CJ was Valerie's most important assignment. She longed to tell him how she felt and to show him her sketches. Today might be the day.

An unaccustomed earthy fragrance filled my nose. I wanted to know what it was. My lazy eyes slowly opened and there was Valerie in the flowers with all her cascading beauty. Her hair brushed my face as she leaned over to prop up my pillow. Without thinking, my fingers signed. Her bluest eyes almost popped out of her startled face as her fingers replied.

An inhaled gasp filled the room. When Valerie moved backwards, other faces came into view. Propped up by my wearied father, mother wept. What I couldn't believe my eyes. Mr. Andros walked right into the room. He wore a small black cap on his head and carried a Bible. I wondered what he was doing here. Without a word, he approached my bed.

"CJ everything is going to be fine. You've been on a rather long trip and we're so glad that you're back."

"But Mr. Andros what about the farm, the ring?"

"So you did hear me. All my boyhood stories about the farm. I knew that you heard me." The little box tumbled right out of his hand and popped open. A beautiful silver ring stared back at me. "I hope it fits."

"But this isn't the wedding ring."

"No it's a ring for you, God's ring of cherished love, so you will never get lost again. CJ, I have visited you for months and knew all along that you would come back home."

My parents burst. "Rabbi, thank you for all of your daily prayers for our boy. God answered them."

"Mr. Andros, you're a Rabbi, a Jewish Rabbi? Then you know the songs the ones I know?"

"Yes, I brought my guitar and sung to you. I'm so glad that you remembered them."

"Remember them? They are the most beautiful songs that I have ever heard. I played them on my violin with Rabbi, the one who lost his son.

Mother do you remember? He returned to Israel because the government agents took away his home, which was our home as well. The snow, the ice, the cold, the fear, the streets . . . . Mother you do remember the tunnel?"

Victoria trembled visibly as she held me in her stricken arms. Her eyes said it all. Here is my beloved son wanting me so to remember his dreams. I must stop him from slipping back into those imaginations. No stranger's hand will ever take him away from me again.

Mother spoke quietly. "CJ everything will fall back into place. Your mind just needs to rest." Utterly confused, I lay back and tried to make sense of it all. Mother's styled hair and manicured painted nails were perfect, not one hair was out of place nor one nail chipped. She had not been fixing food or cleaning cafeterias. How did Dad ever get out of the nursing home? I was told he never made it. Mr. Andros wasn't in love with my mother. He never even looked twice at her. He was in love with God. Valerie was beautiful as ever, but older and dressed in a candy striper's uniform. My in and out thoughts were interrupted by a small parade of kids. Grinning baseball players from school were shadowed by smaller kids. My eyes froze. The tunnel kids were in my room.

"CJ we've been teaching these inner- city kids how to play baseball. We needed your help." There's a kid here who wants to become a catcher." Little Sam and I stared at each other.

"Let me see your arms." He hesitated.

"They're skinny." He slowly rolled up his sleeves and they were skinny with no marks, no cuts, no scars, just a regular pair of arms.

"Where do you live?"

"In the city with my other brothers. We don't have very much to eat, or fancy clothes, but we have baseball. Near our school, there was an old abandoned field where we practiced. Stones were bases. One day, your friends joined us and taught us how real baseball was played. A catcher was all that I wanted to be. They said you were the best. Will you teach me? I have waited for you to wake up so I could ask you man to man." The way Sam talked, those expressions, I remembered them. He was the Sam I knew but without the fear, the pain.

The other boys wanted a turn. One by one, each boy stepped forward to take a good look at me. "We never thought that we would actually be able to talk to you. You were always asleep. Your friends insisted that we share our love of baseball with you. After every game, we came right over and let you know exactly what did and didn't happen."

"Say where exactly do you live?"

"In the city, near the abandoned tunnels. The tunnels are our forts. Nobody can find us and we stay in there as long as we want. Sometimes homeless people run us out. My foot got infected the other week when I stepped on an old discarded needle. It went right through my toe. There's an older man who everybody calls . . ."

"Wait don't tell me. The colonel, the tunnel master."

"Yes that's right. Everyone is scared of him except for me. His mind is gone. He cussed and cried at the same time. I tried to talk to him but he insisted he was a lost coal miner. He pulled a knife out of his shirt and stuck it in a rock and cut himself. That was the last time I saw him.

You know long ago, there used to be a lot of underground construction in our area, mining. Everybody thought the land was valuable. It wasn't. When my dad lost his job, he left. Never saw him again not once. The good doc told me that if I tried hard enough I could wake you up. Do you remember anything that I told you about my band, how much I love to play the electric guitar and sing? About the other kids who thought we were rock stars and just loved to be around us. Without the music, we were eaten up and spit out by poverty. Some rich guy felt sorry for us and bought us some supped up equipment. Now people ask us to play, the gigs you know."

"Did you know that Valerie was one of your fans?"

"The looker who works here? Well sure she sits in all the time. I don't know why she can't hear much. Her ears were messed up. But she sure turns heads." The more I listened it began to make more sense. Some of these kids talked to me for months so I guess I became part of their lives.

"Your name's Eric right?"

"Yeah, how did you know?"

"You just reminded me of somebody. But there was still one unanswered question. How did I get like this? My Dad had the only possible answer.

My dad reached for my hands and held them to his chest. "Son, some of this may scare you a little but don't let it. I wanted to make sure you had your footing before I told you."

"Well my feet are here if that's what you mean."

"Do you remember that critical baseball game the one that qualified your team for the championship? During that game you got knocked out and hit very hard in the sweet spot of your brain, an unprotected part that left you more than unconscious. You went into a comma and we couldn't reach you. All the prayers in the world didn't work so we reached out to many others. Everyday, there have been kids from school in here talking to you about anything and everything. You spoke in Hebrew so we contacted a Rabbi who sifted through your words, always fighting, always angry, beaten, lost, but always with mother. I was never mentioned."

"Mother never wanted me to find you. But I found you. You were all crumpled up. You couldn't talk. When you looked at me, you howled like an animal. My love for you had no place to go. I ran and ran just wanted to die so we could always be together. I couldn't make it without you: Mother tried her best to take your place but couldn't. You're my dad, my hope, the other mitt that fits my glove. You made me feel so special, the most important thing to you. I just kept fighting Dad. I couldn't stop. My dad grabbed me and couldn't let me go. His uncontrollable tears weren't wiped away.

"CJ, man to man, I give you my word that nothing in this world will ever separate me from you again. You can be sure that I will never miss another baseball game." With my dad's hand in mine, I felt another hand.

My God, my Father in Heaven, his hand was joined with mine. My God and I together broke through the camouflage, the lies, the deception. I would never again be that wealthy, selfish, stuck-up kid who thought that life revolved around me. God opened my heart; it would never again be made of stone. I now knew what love was. Love for mother and dad. Love for others who were different. Love for those who had nothing. Love for the discarded, the forgotten. My life was returned to me. It would glorify God. Grateful eyes closed as I hummed a Hebrew song praising God who led me back. Fearless sleep beckoned me.

Printed in the United States
By Bookmasters